I0760723

THE LIAR

THE MESSES, BOOK THREE

KIERSTEN MODGLIN

Cover Design by Kiersten Modglin
Copy Editing by Three Owls Editing
Formatting by Kiersten Modglin

First Print and Electronic Edition: 2018
kierstenmodglinauthor.com

In loving memory of my Aunt Marilyn Reed.
For always supporting and loving me.
I love and miss you every day.
10/5/1951-10/8/2018

ONE

FLETCHER

Fletcher Denali's life began the moment that it ended. At least that's what he'd always believed...until the day he met her. From the moment he laid eyes on Vaida Williams, he knew he hadn't been living. Not really. Not yet. She was the first girl to make him look twice since Holly.

"Fletcher," Burt called from behind him, making him jump up and bang his head on the inside of the stove he'd been cleaning.

"Oh, shit, ouch. Yeah?" He spun around, clutching his head. Burt stood in front of him, next to a woman he'd never seen before. She smiled at him, her dark eyes glowing next to her caramel skin.

"Hi," he said, smiling through the radiating pain in his head. He pulled his hand away, checking to make sure there was no blood before he offered it up to the girl. She shook it cautiously.

"Fletch, this is Vaida. Vaida, Fletcher Denali. He takes care of everything around here, so if you have any questions, he's your guy. Fletcher, I want you to show her the ropes around this place."

"Okay, no problem," Fletcher agreed, throwing the grease-covered towel over his shoulder. With that, Burt walked away, leaving them alone. "Welcome to the madhouse," Fletcher joked, watching as her eyes scanned the room before landing back on him.

"That bad?" she asked, baring her teeth in a grimace.

He waved a hand. "Nah, Burt's a good boss. The rest of the guys here are pretty cool, too."

She didn't look entirely convinced as she ran a finger across the countertop. "Okay, good." She bobbed her head. "Well, put me to work."

He nodded, handing her a clean cloth from above their heads. Any of the other guys would've put her on the stove and taken the easy job for themselves, but Fletcher couldn't make himself do it. "We're in between rushes right now, so I'm just trying to clean up a bit. You can start by wiping down all the counters." He handed her a bottle of sanitizing spray.

"Okay," she said, turning and beginning to spray the stainless steel countertops. He got on his knees, stuck his head back into the oven, and began scrubbing the caked on food again. He was strangely conscious of how he looked, trying to angle himself in an attractive way though this was hardly a sexy job.

"So, are you from around here, Vaida?" he asked, his voice echoing from inside the oven.

"No," she said simply, not bothering to elaborate.

"What brings you to Burt's, then? A love of greasy food and long hours?" he teased.

"No," she said again. "I just...needed a change. My roommate knows Burt; he helped me get the job."

"Your roommate?" he asked, sliding out of the stove and wiping his hands off. "Anyone I might know?"

She was quiet for a moment. "It's a big city, Fletcher. Do you really think you know every person?" Her voice was almost cold.

"Sorry," he said, leaning back in and scrubbing away again. He'd obviously offended her somehow. Small talk had never been his forté. "I'm not trying to sound nosey. It just gets quiet around here. I'll shut up."

When she spoke again, several minutes had passed, and it almost shocked him to hear her voice. "I don't mean to be rude. I'm just...I don't like to talk about myself."

Now, that was something he at least understood. "Hey, you don't owe me an apology. I was just making small talk." He couldn't help his clipped tone.

"How long have you worked here?" she asked.

"Not too long. Just since last fall." When she didn't respond, he peeked out of the stove, watching her scrub the countertops. She was slow, methodical, and he was mesmerized by her movements. Her shoulder-length, black hair was tied in a loose ponytail at the nape of her neck. The blue jeans she wore wrapped tightly around her curves, and the black t-shirt lifted up when she leaned over too far to reveal a small sliver of her light brown skin.

She stopped moving, looking over her shoulder at him. "Am I doing something wrong?"

"What? No." He looked away quickly. "No, you're doing fine."

She nodded, her brow furrowed as if she were thinking hard. "So, are *you* from here, then? Atlanta, I mean."

"Nah," he said, catching himself before he told too much of the truth. "I'm from all over."

"Ahh, so you're an Army brat?"

"No, just a brat in general."

She let out a small laugh. "You're a funny guy, huh?"

"I do what I can," he said, a cocky grin spreading on his face. "So, have you settled in yet? Made some friends?"

"*Made some friends?* What, like we're in kindergarten?" She snorted. "No, not really. Why? Are you offering?"

He stood up, dusting off his knees. "Well, if you insist. I'm pretty familiar with Atlanta at this point, at least. I could take you to a party, introduce you to a few people. Have you feeling right at home."

"Thanks, but I'm all right," she said, her smile sad. She looked at the cloth in her hand. "I appreciate the offer though."

"Sure, anytime." He looked down, then back up, unable to deny the disappointment he felt. "It's a standing invitation," he told her, kicking himself for sounding so desperate to get to know her.

"I'll keep that in mind," she said, starting to scrub the counter again. "Thanks, Fletcher."

He nodded, trying to stop staring at her, though it was growing increasingly difficult to pull his eyes away.

TWO

FLETCHER

Fletcher drove to the small psychiatric clinic where Fiona was living. It had been a few months since they'd transferred her there. The place seemed nice enough, and it should be for the small fortune it was costing him monthly, though they'd never let him past the entryway to see for himself. He carried a bundle of flowers—something to spruce up her room. She'd always loved daffodils.

He walked into the building, through the set of metal detectors, and up to the glass window. The receptionist greeted him immediately.

"Hello, how can I help you?"

"I'm here to see Fiona Denali," he said, pulling out his wallet.

Before he could reach for his ID, she typed something into her computer, her eyes scanning the screen. "I'm sorry," she said, shaking her head. "But I'm afraid that's not going to be possible."

"Why not?" he asked, already knowing the answer. Since he'd chosen to move her from the small hospital to the clinic—a more permanent facility—she'd been refusing to see him. The clinic only allowed visitors twice a week, and it was hard enough to find time to get there with his work schedule. To drive an hour across town just to be turned away was getting infuriating.

"I'm sorry. It doesn't say." She squinted, staring at the screen again, searching for an answer.

"Well, if you don't know, can you find someone who does? I mean, you have to tell me something. Please. I can't keep driving out here for her to refuse to see me. It's not exactly a short trip, and I'm having to miss work to be here. I know that she's mad at me, but I want to see her. I don't think that's too much to ask."

Just then, a nurse he recognized appeared behind the receptionist. "Fletcher?" she asked, looking shocked to see him. "Is everything all right?"

"Yeah, er, no," he responded. "You're one of Fi's nurses, right? Can you tell me what's going on with her? I haven't been allowed to see her in months."

She nodded, reading the computer screen over the woman's shoulder before looking up. "Come with me please," she instructed, opening the door and allowing him to pass through. Her face was solemn as he walked past the doors and took a seat in a set of chairs across from where she sat down.

"What's going on?" he asked. "Why can't I see her?"

She took a breath. "Fletcher, I'm so sorry you've been

unable to see her lately. Fiona isn't well right now. I would've thought someone would have called you."

He shook his head, glancing down at his phone. "I haven't gotten any calls. What do you mean she isn't well?"

"She..." She hesitated, looking down at her hands. "We had another suicide attempt." She held her hands up, trying to calm the panic she must've seen in his eyes. "She's okay. We investigated, of course, and found out who gave her the pills. They have been separated. Things like this don't happen often, but we can't always avoid them, I'm afraid. We're doing everything we can to protect Fiona from herself, and right now that means not allowing any outside contact."

"I'm paying for her to be here, and you're telling me I can't even see her? How do I know she's being taken care of? How do I know she's not sick or in worse shape than when I brought her here? I just want to see her—talk to her for a second. I don't need a full visit, but you've got to give me something."

The nurse smiled stiffly. "I understand your concerns. I need you to trust me when I say it's in Fiona's best interest that she's not in contact with anyone aside from her doctor and team of nurses right now. You chose this place because of our reputation. Because of what we can do for Fiona and others like her. I can assure you we're taking excellent care of her. I know this must be hard for you. And I know it's not the news you were hoping for."

"For how long? How long until I can see her?" he asked, his jaw tight.

"That's not up to me. But you can rest assured that it's top priority for us to get Fiona stable enough to make contact with her family and friends. I promise you we are working toward that every day."

"Is she okay? Like, really okay?" he asked, feeling a lump forming in his throat.

"She's okay, Fletcher, honestly." She spoke slowly. "She is, but she needs time."

He rubbed his jaw. "I'm all she has."

The nurse pressed her lips together. "That's not true. And, more than that, it's not healthy."

"What?" he asked, staring at her.

"I'm concerned that what you mean is *she's* all *you* have."

He shook his head. "What are you talking about?"

"You're a good brother," she told him, patting his hand. "You've been amazing throughout this process and that's exactly what Fiona needs. But, I can't help wondering..." She trailed off, looking uneasy.

"Wondering what?" he demanded.

"I'm wondering...what is it that *you* need, Fletcher? Or have you gone so long focusing on Fiona's care that you've forgotten?"

THREE

FLETCHER

"Can I get those fries for table fourteen?" Vaida's voice came from behind him.

"Waffle?"

She spoke loudly over the fryer's hum. "No, seasoned."

"Oh, right. There you go." He scooped the fries into the basket. "And here's eighteen's burger. No cheese, extra pickles."

She smiled, taking them both. "Thank you." He nodded, facing the fryer again in time to pull out the next batch.

Burt appeared from his office. "Fletcher, we out of bananas?" he asked, scratching his balding head.

Fletcher nodded without having to check. "Used the last of our shipment this morning. I think we're going to need to start ordering double. Second week in a row we've run out. Those new shakes are killing us."

Burt grumbled. "Guess I'll call and see about getting an extra delivery—"

"Already done," Fletcher interrupted, flipping the sole burger left on the grill. "They'll have it to us tomorrow before we open. It was the soonest they could squeeze us in."

"You're the best, kid," Burt responded, sounding relieved.

"Doesn't help us today, though," Fletcher said before Burt could walk away.

"Right," Burt said, scratching his head again. "Well, I guess I can run down and grab some from the market."

Fletcher pulled the burger from the grill, placed it on a bun, and added extra everything for one of their regulars. He handed it to Vaida. "Doug," he told her as she took the basket and headed for his table.

"I mean, I can run out if you need me to," Fletcher told his boss who was still lingering in the doorway. "Lunch is dying down. I guess Vaida can handle it for a few minutes."

"Where's Jaxon?" Burt glanced around the diner.

"Called out."

"Evan?"

"His daughter has that *thing* today, remember?"

"So, it's just been you two all day?" He looked bewildered.

"Um, yeah, Burt, but we've got this." Fletcher wiped the top of the ketchup and mustard bottles and turned down the fryer.

"Jesus, I would've come out to help if I'd known, Fletch."

"No biggie," Vaida said, coming back into the conversation with a wave of her hand. "It hasn't been too bad."

"Okay," Burt said with a sigh. "Well, I guess you guys

can manage if I run out for a bit then, right? To get some bananas, I mean."

Fletcher held in his laughter. "Yeah, I think we've got it from here, Burt."

He smiled sarcastically, speeding past the two of them. "I'll be back. Don't burn the place down."

Once he was out the door, Vaida leaned against the counter, gripping it with both hands. "Do you think he even notices that you run the show around here?" she asked.

"Nah," he said, shrugging. "It's easy to make it seem that way, I guess. Burt still does a lot."

"I don't know about that." She ran the toe of her shoe along the lines of the black and white tile.

"What about you? You're like a little diner rockstar," he joked, nudging her.

She rolled her eyes. "Waiting tables isn't exactly rocket science."

He held up his spatula, miming flipping a burger. "Yeah, well, for the record, grilling burgers isn't either. But, it's easy enough and we make decent tips." Plus, Burt being willing to pay in cash made this one of the only jobs he could safely acquire. But, of course, he couldn't say that out loud.

"So, what do you do when you aren't working, Fletcher?"

"Nothing," he said simply. "I'm pretty boring. What about you?"

"Same," she said, lowering her brow. "I thought you said you had friends here."

He shook his head. "I never said that. I mean, the guys here, I guess, but they're more acquaintances than friends."

"My first day here you invited me to a party with you

and your friends." She smirked, her lips pressed into a thin line.

"Yeah," he said with a sigh, "and if you'd said yes, I would've had to find a party pretty quick." He looked up at the ceiling, his face burning.

She snorted, covering her nose. What was it about her that was so endearing? Fletcher found that everything she did just gave him further reason to want to know her better. "You invited me to a party that didn't exist?"

He squinted his eyes, nodding his head slowly. "Yeah, I kind of did." He whipped the towel in her direction playfully. "But, if you'd said yes, I would've found you a kickass party, even if I had to throw it myself."

"Well, if I'd known you were going through all that trouble, maybe I would've gone," she teased.

"You definitely should've." She laughed, reaching over and grabbing a handful of straws to refill her apron pocket. "What about you? What do you do when you aren't here? Besides 'nothing'? What do you like to do for fun?"

Her eyes looked tired. "To be honest, I haven't been able to have fun in years, Fletcher. So, I wouldn't know."

"Years? I don't believe that. Everyone has to have a little fun sometimes." He stared at her, trying to decipher her expression.

"I like to bake," she said thoughtfully. "And I like music. I wanted to be a singer when I was young."

"What changed?"

"I grew up," she said, her mouth barely moving, eyes lost to her thoughts.

"You are still pretty young, Vaida. Way too young to be so jaded."

She shook her head. "Age speaks nothing to experience."

"Meaning?" Her words hit him hard, and he finally saw a darkness behind her expression he realized must've been there all along. It was a darkness he could connect with all too well.

She turned away, no longer facing him when she answered. "Just that I grew up long before I was grown."

FOUR

FLETCHER

The next day, Fletcher and Jaxon walked into their favorite pizza place, a small restaurant across from their apartment called Leo's.

"Hey," Jaxon whispered, "look who it is." He pointed across the room to where Vaida was sitting alone, a slice of half-eaten pizza in front of her.

"Huh," Fletcher said, trying to act casual.

"Should we go sit with her? Doesn't look like she's with anyone," Jaxon coaxed.

"I don't know, man. She may not want to be bothered," Fletcher said uneasily.

"Don't be ridiculous," Jaxon said, approaching the table where she was sitting. His usual carefree vibe made Fletcher jealous. Jaxon never worried about anything—least of all embarrassing himself in front of a girl he was crazy about. "Hey, Vaida."

She looked up, pulling the cheese strings from her pizza. "Oh, hey guys," she said, rubbing her fingers on a napkin. She tucked a piece of hair behind her ear. "What are you doing here?"

"What are *you* doing here is more like it? We're here every week," Jaxon informed her.

She smiled, her eyes darting to meet Fletcher's. "Oh. Am I in your seat or something, then?"

"No," Fletcher said, reassuring her. "We just wanted to say hello."

"I'm going to grab our pizza," Jaxon said. "You two wait here." As he walked away, he winked at Fletcher over Vaida's shoulder. "Be right back."

Fletcher rolled his eyes, looking back at Vaida. "I'm sorry if we interrupted. Jaxon is...persistent."

"No, not at all," she said. "It's good to see you. Both of you," she added. "What, ah, what are you guys up to?"

He shrugged, leaning against the table top. "We come here for pizza on our days off. Jaxon used to work here, so Leo gives him a good discount."

"I didn't realize you two were close," she said, raising an eyebrow as she took a small bite of her pizza.

"Well, we're roommates."

"Oh," she said, obviously waiting for him to go on.

"Yeah, he rents me his second bedroom. He's an okay guy, you know. Most of the guys at Burt's are—"

"Different," she said with a laugh.

"That's putting it lightly," he agreed. "But, yeah, Jaxon's one of the better one's there."

"I wondered how you ended up in a place like that."

"It's a job," he told her, sliding into the chair across from her.

"You don't mind all the crap Burt puts you through? I mean, I barely see you with any days off the schedule. And when you are there, you're pulling more weight than anyone."

"I need the money," he said simply.

"For what? An expensive coke addiction?" she asked, her eyes warm. He swallowed hard, not responding. Her jaw dropped. "Geeze, Fletcher, I'm sorry. I was only joking." She stared at him in horror, reading his guarded expression. "It's none of my business anyway."

"No, it's fine," he said. "I don't have an addiction. It's...family stuff. I'm taking care of my sister. She's pretty sick, and the responsibility has kind of fallen to me. Her treatment isn't cheap."

She covered her mouth. "I'm so sorry to hear that, Fletcher. God, now I feel like such a jerk. I shouldn't have said anything."

"It's fine, Vaida. Don't worry about it, honestly. You didn't know. I just...I don't really like to talk about it."

"Totally understand," she said quickly. "Really, I do." She paused. "Well, anyway, I should be going."

He stared at the slice of pizza she'd hardly touched since he arrived. "Don't let me run you off. I can take a hint."

She frowned. "You aren't. I just severely underestimated how big these slices would be. I'll let you guys get back to your fun." She stood up, dusted off her hands, and dropped her plate in a nearby trash can as she hurried out the door with a slight wave over her shoulder.

"You let her go?" Jaxon asked, approaching the table with their pizza.

"I'm an idiot," Fletcher said with a sigh.

"So, go get her, man."

"No way. I'm not bailing on you."

"*Puh-lease.* You've been talking about that girl ever since the day she started. Besides, if you don't go after her, I will. I'm not going to let you have dibs forever."

Fletcher could've hugged him. He tried to reign in his smile. "You're sure?"

"Go," Jaxon insisted, forcing a piece of pizza in his mouth and sitting down. Not having to be told again, Fletcher dashed out of the restaurant, searching for her on the crowded street. He caught a glimpse of her green t-shirt.

"Vaida," he shouted, starting to jog in her direction. She heard him the second time he called for her and spun around to search the crowd. He hurried to her, waving his hand to catch her eye.

"Did I forget something?" she asked, a hand over her brow to shield her eyes from the sun.

"No," he said, breathing heavily when he reached her. "I just wanted to catch up with you." She stared at him, waiting for him to say more, and he tried to think on his feet. He hadn't come up with a plan for if he actually managed to catch her. "Do you, uh, want to go grab a bite to eat or something?"

She raised her eyebrows, looking amused. "Um, I just ate."

"Shit. Right. Um, yeah. Well, right." He paused, collecting his thoughts. She made his head spin, jumbling his thoughts.

"But," she said, saving him from further embarrassment, "I was thinking of going for a walk before I head home. Would you like to join me?"

He smiled. "That'd be great."

She wrinkled her nose. "It's not a date or anything, right?"

"Would it be that bad if I said it was?"

She hesitated, touching her lip. "I'm just not sure that would be such a good idea. You know, with working together and everything."

"Fine. I'll quit then," he said with a smirk.

She snorted, covering her mouth. "Trust me, I'm not worth all that."

He put his hands in his pockets. "You shouldn't say that. It seems like you're worth quite a lot to me." *Did he just insinuate that she was a hooker?* He groaned internally, trying not to let her see his stress. What on earth did this woman do to him?

She shook her head. "Fletcher, if you know what's smart, you'll stay far away from me."

"Lucky for both of us, I never said I was smart. It's my good looks that get me through life," he told her. "And trust me, if we're talking about bad decisions, I'm not the best choice for you either." He nudged her with his elbow. "If that makes you feel any better."

"Oh, great," she said sarcastically, a bright smile on her face.

He laughed. "But, I'm a lot of fun."

"Just last week you told me you were pretty boring."

He touched his chin, grinning. "Okay, I'm not that fun either. Why are you going out with me again?"

She looked down at the sidewalk. "I never said I was."

He held out a hand for hers. "Well, maybe I am boring, but I do believe you told me you weren't very exciting either. Maybe that makes us a match made in heaven."

She nodded. "That's a scary thought." As she turned down the next street, she took his outstretched hand carefully. Something happened as their skin connected, a spark Fletcher hadn't felt since Holly. It was a fire within him he'd been unsure he'd ever experience again. He'd spent so much of his life with other people, first Fiona, then Holly. Since losing them both, he'd spent months on end feeling incredibly lost and alone. But, something about Vaida made him feel different. Better. He knew then, holding her hand and feeling the unfamiliar warmth in the pit of his stomach, he'd do anything and everything to make sure Vaida became his.

"So, where do you live?" he asked. "Near here?"

She frowned. "No, not really."

He groaned, shaking his head. "Always the mystery, Vaida."

They passed a small hole-in-the-wall bar where Fletcher had played guitar at a few open mic nights before. "Hey, let's run in here. You said you aren't hungry, but you didn't say anything about drinks."

She glanced at her phone. "It's not even three."

"They have soda, Vaida. What are you? An alcoholic?" he joked. She smiled, shaking her head. He loved her smile—the way it lit up her whole face made him smile without thought. "This place is super low-key, trust me."

She pressed her lips together. "Okay," she said hesitantly.

He turned around, leading her through the door and to

the back corner of the bar. The place was mostly empty, as the evening crowd hadn't hit yet. They had music playing from the overhead speakers, but no other distinguishable noise could be heard. A pretty waitress with purple hair and thick rimmed glasses approached them. "What can I get y'all?"

"Just a Coke for me," Vaida said.

"Sweet tea here," Fletcher said with a nod.

The waitress disappeared, coming back a few moments later with their drinks. Vaida stuck a straw in hers immediately, taking a sip. "Thank you," she said to the waitress before she walked away.

"So," Fletcher said once she was out of earshot, "tell me about yourself, Vaida."

"You know me," she said shyly.

"No, I don't. Honestly, I don't know you at all. Where are you from?" he asked, taking a drink of his tea. It wasn't nearly sweet enough.

"I'm from a city a few miles south of here," she answered vaguely.

"No kidding? Me too," he said, catching himself before he gave away his true hometown rather than his cover story. He was supposed to be from Tennessee, not Georgia.

She nodded. "Mine's very small."

"Do you have family there?"

"No," she said, "not anymore."

"I'm sorry to hear that."

"What about you?"

"Family?" he asked. She nodded. "I have a brother and a sister. One lives back home, the other lives here in Atlanta."

"Must be nice, having someone close."

"Yeah, I guess so," he mumbled, scratching his bicep. "I don't know. We don't see each other very often anymore."

"Trouble in paradise?" she asked, twirling her straw in her glass mindlessly.

"It's complicated, I guess. Dark pasts and lots of secrets," he said with a smirk. He wasn't sure why he was being so honest with her, though he'd tried to play it off as a joke. His cardinal rule was to never talk about himself, but he couldn't seem to keep the words from spewing out when he was around her.

"Oh, I know all about those." She raised her eyebrows, her gaze faltering.

"I figured as much."

She looked up at him suddenly. "What?"

"I mean, from one person on the run to the other, I know the signs. You're quiet, you answer every question with less than a sentence. Plus, I did payroll for Burt last week. I'd always thought I was one of the only people he paid in cash, but then you came along. You don't want to be found, Vaida." He stared at her. "Dark pasts and secrets, right?"

She stared at him, her expression growing fearful, though she seemed to be trying to stay calm. "You don't know what you're talking about."

He nodded. "I do," he said, taking another drink. "But, don't worry. If my secret's safe with you, you can trust me with yours."

She frowned. "I don't have a secret, Fletcher. I don't know what you think you know, but you've got it all wrong."

He fiddled with his crumpled straw paper, leaning back in his seat. "Okay," he said, holding his hands up in defeat. "You're probably right. Forget I said anything."

She nodded, moving to stand up. "I should go."

"Wait, Vaida," he begged. "Don't go. I honestly didn't mean to upset you. I promise I don't mean any harm. Whatever you do or don't have to hide is one hundred percent your business. I'm sorry if I overstepped. We all have secrets. I'm just letting you know you have a friend. You know, if you ever need one."

"I don't," she answered quickly, but then lowered her voice. "But, thank you."

"Don't go," he said again. "We just got here."

"Yeah, I know. I really should get going, Fletcher. I'm sorry."

"What about a dance, then? One dance?" he offered, hope filling his chest.

"A dance?" She looked around the mostly empty bar. "Are you joking?"

"Of course not," he assured her, standing up. She didn't stop him when he took her hand, wrapping his arm around her waist and beginning to sway to the soft music.

"You realize we're the only ones in the whole bar dancing, right?" she asked. The few patrons of the quiet bar were staring at them strangely.

"I mean, we're also the only ones falling in love in the whole bar," he said, a confident smile on his face.

She reeled back. "Now I know you're crazy. I don't know you, Fletcher. I'm sure not falling in love with you."

He stared into her almond-colored eyes. "Well, I guess I'm going to have to up my game, then, aren't I?"

She furrowed her brow. "Fletcher, I'm not going to fall in love with you." Their bodies were pressed together, their voices low, but her face told him she was serious. "Not today. Not ever."

He shrugged. "I'll just have to change your mind, then. I like a challenge."

She scowled. "Why are you single anyway?"

"You mean because I'm so attractive and totally dateable?"

A fake laugh escaped her mouth. "Ah, I see why, nevermind."

He grinned, their cheeks brushing, his lips near her ear. "No, in all seriousness, my, um, my fiancée died last year. I haven't dated since."

She stopped dancing, pulling away from him. "Oh, god, Fletcher. I'm so sorry. I had no idea."

He nodded, looking down. He couldn't talk about Holly, not yet. "I know. It's okay."

"Can I ask what happened?"

He thought about it for a moment before responding. "Yes," he said finally, "if I can ask you something in return."

"Deal," she said hesitantly.

"She was murdered. By my sister." He swallowed, feeling exposed.

She took a breath, her face still. "Dark pasts and secrets?" she whispered, not blinking.

He pressed his lips together. "Dark pasts and secrets." He took her back in his arms, moving to the music again. Somehow she was less stiff against him, as if the horror of his past had somehow given them a connection.

"So, what's your question for me? A deal's a deal."

"Hmmm..." he said, thinking out loud. "What do I want to know? How about...your favorite food?"

"What? That's your question?"

He smiled at her, moving a piece of hair from her eyes. "I want to know more about you, Vaida, but I don't want you to tell me because we made a deal. I, of all people, understand keeping secrets to protect those we love. Or ourselves." She stared at him with a dumbfounded expression, leaning back. "See, I told you I'm a friend." He shrugged.

"You're really something, Mr. Denali," she said, her voice awestruck.

"You haven't seen anything yet," he promised, a twinkle in his eye.

"Spaghetti," she said finally, holding eye contact. "My favorite food is spaghetti."

He smiled. "Now, that's information I can use."

FIVE

VAIDA

"Hey, Cody," she said, walking into her apartment and laying down her keys.

"Hey, boo-boo," he called, smiling at her over the back of the couch. "You okay?"

She nodded. "Don't I look it?" She was trying her hardest.

"No," he said in regular Cody fashion with way too much southern twang. "You look like a ragged mess." He paused Netflix, turning back around to face her. "Long day?"

"Actually, no," she answered thoughtfully. "Today was a good day."

"Well, that's a first." He stood up, marching across the living room and setting a wine glass on the counter. "Did you meet a boy?" He batted his eyelashes at her playfully.

"Not technically," she said.

"Technically-*smechnically*, sister. I need the dirty

details." His fingers danced together in front of his chin as if he were devising an evil plot. "Lord knows I haven't seen a dick in two months. Let me live vicariously through you."

Her face grew warm, still not quite used to Cody's brutal honesty and total inability to filter himself. "I'm afraid it's pretty uneventful. I just ran into a guy from work."

"And?" He wiggled his thick eyebrows.

"And nothing. We went to a bar and drank a soda. Nothing spectacular."

Cody scoffed. "Hot guys are wasted on you, Vaida."

"Who said he's hot?"

He pointed to her guilty grin. "Would you be smiling like that if he wasn't?"

She shook her head, looking away from him. "It doesn't matter. It was just one afternoon. I'm not going to do anything about it."

"And why not?" He pouted.

"Because my life is way too busy to deal with a relationship." She folded her arms across her chest.

"Honey, I've seen your schedule." He counted her tasks on his fingers, looking skeptical. "Sleeping, showering, more sleeping, shifts at the diner, large amounts of time spent avoiding my questions, and going to the gym twice a week. You aren't *that* busy."

She let out a small laugh. "You forgot about Netflix binging."

He eyed the television. "Yeah, I may have started without you."

"I noticed."

"Well, sue me. You were out drinking with your man-candy. I got bored."

She rolled her eyes, grabbed a glass from the cabinet above her head, and poured herself some wine. "Well, maybe if you got off the couch and went outside—" He gasped, looking appalled at the mere suggestion. "You would meet some man-candy of your own," she finished.

"First of all, *the outside* is full of nasty boys. No, thank you. I'll stick to my phone and *Drop Dead Diva.* Second of all, are you admitting he's man-candy? Or admitting he's yours? Or maybe admitting both?"

She groaned. "He's cute, sure." She tried desperately to hold back the smile that was growing on her face.

He pursed his lips. "*Cute* is for puppy dogs, baby. Let's look him up. I wanna see this guy." She took a sip of her wine, waiting. "Well, get on Facebook, girl," he said, one hand on his hip. "What are you waiting for?"

"You know I don't do social media," she said.

He shook his head. "You are nuts. Facebook shouldn't even count as social media. It's like...the fourth basic need. Right after water."

"Before sex?" she asked playfully.

"Honey, if you do it right, it's all just foreplay." She giggled, watching Cody pull out his phone. "Oh, fine. I'll look him up. What's his name?" he asked.

"Fletcher," she told him. "Fletcher Denali." She remembered the name that Burt had given her, though she couldn't be sure of the spelling.

He stared at his phone, his thumbs scrolling down the screen. "Is this him?" he asked, holding the phone out. Vaida shook her head. He pulled it back to him, scrolling again. "Ew, it better not be him," he said, still scrolling. "I don't see a Fletcher Denali in Atlanta."

She bit her lip, remembering what he'd said about not wanting to be found. "Well, maybe he's not on Facebook either."

"Ew, sweetie," Cody said, looking concerned. "Is he *old?* Saggy balls are not good. Trust me on this."

She frowned, taking another drink. "He's *not* old."

"Then, he's on Facebook," he insisted. "Trust me on that, too."

"I'm not old and I'm also not on Facebook," she said testily.

He narrowed his eyes at her. "Point taken," he replied. "But, you are also a little strange."

She walked away from him, sitting down on the couch and throwing a blanket over her legs. "Regardless, I'm not going to date him. So, whether he's cute or not makes no difference."

"But, for the record..." Cody pleaded, not giving up.

"He's not bad," she admitted, her smile growing larger as her face heated up.

He crossed his arms, a devilish glare in his eyes. "Not bad? Coming from you, he must be sex on legs."

"Is that all you think about?"

He flopped on the couch beside her. "Of course not," he said. "I think about wine too. Oh, and my hair. Oh my god, and Netflix. Speaking of, you'll never guess what Kim did on the last episode. I'll restart it." He grabbed the remote with a sly grin. "See, sex is just like...ninety-eight percent of what's up there. I'm not an animal."

SIX

FLETCHER

"Well, good morning," Fletcher said when Vaida walked into the diner for their next shift together. He hadn't stopped thinking about her in the forty-eight hours since he'd seen her last.

"Morning," she said casually while strolling past him with a sideways glance.

"How've you been?" he asked, following her to the register as she clocked in.

She held up the paper coffee cup in her hand. "Fine."

"You know we have coffee here, right?"

"My apartment offers it for free. No biggie."

He smiled. "You look nice today."

She looked down at herself as if she didn't believe him. "Thanks," she said finally. "You too. Has it been busy here?"

"Nah, not too bad so far."

"Morning, Vaida," Aidan sang as he hurried past them.

"Morning," she said with a smile.

"What time do you get off later?" Fletcher asked, watching Aidan go.

"Me?" Vaida asked.

"Yes, you," he said, looking back at her with a smile. "Of course you."

"Three," she said with a frown. "You?"

"I'm leaving in an hour," he told her. "Maybe we could do something tonight?" He leaned back on the counter, trying to appear more calm than he felt. He was severely out of practice at this.

"What did you have in mind?" she asked, throwing her coffee cup away as she began tying her black apron around her waist.

"I don't know. I was thinking maybe we could go out to eat? Somewhere nicer than Leo's."

She smiled shyly. "Is this like a date?"

"Yes," he said. "It's exactly like a date." She looked behind him, where he guessed someone might be watching them, but he didn't care. Vaida was too important to him to worry about his stupid pride.

She surprised him by answering quickly. "Okay, yeah. I'd like that."

"Really?" He had expected to have to convince her.

"Sure."

In his pocket, his phone began buzzing. He pulled it out. "Okay, awesome. Cool. Yeah. Excuse me just a sec," he said. "Sorry." He stepped to the back, slipping into the walk-in cooler. "Hello?" he called into the phone.

"Gav, it's me," his brother's voice rang over the line.

"Gunner? What's wrong?" Though they were on

speaking terms for the first time in years, they certainly didn't call each other often. Fletcher knew something was wrong the second he'd seen the number.

Gunner hesitated, taking a sharp breath. "It's...it's Mom —er, Misty. She's dead."

Fletcher stared into space without responding, wondering if this was all some bad dream. He'd had these dreams before, ones where Misty had finally died, only to wake up and find out she was still out there somewhere. He rubbed his forehead, squeezing his eyes shut. "Oh," he said finally.

"I didn't know whether to call. I wasn't really sure if you'd want to know, but—"

"I wanted to know," Fletcher interrupted him. "I needed to. I'm glad you called."

Gunner sighed. "Okay. Well, they're, uh, we're...the service will be tomorrow. I'm just having it at the graveside. Me and Reagan. I don't expect you to come. I don't even want to be there myself, truth be told, but I think someone should."

"Yeah, I don't know," he said, placing his head on the cool metal wall in front of him.

"I know. I don't blame you if you don't come. I just wanted you to know it's over. All of it. If any good comes of this, at least it's that you finally know you're free." Fletcher thought of his sister, then. *Their* sister. Gia, now called Fiona, who would likely spend the rest of her life in a solid white room because of the woman who'd raised them.

"It's not over, Gun. I don't think it'll ever be over. Not for us." He paused. "Was she alone? When it happened? Was she alone?"

"Yeah," Gunner answered. "She was in the hospital, but she was alone. Her doctor found her Tuesday morning."

Fletcher swallowed. "Good."

"You okay, man? I can come up if I need to."

"No," Fletcher said quickly. "No, I'm fine. Thanks."

"Okay," Gunner said awkwardly. "Well, I'll see you around then, I guess."

"Yeah," Fletcher grumbled. "Yeah, I'll see you around." He pressed the red button on his screen, turning and slamming his hands on the wire rack beside him. A bag of cheese fell to the ground, and he bent over to grab it, cursing. He was surprised to feel tears stinging his eyes, but he knew they must be from the cold. His chest felt tight, his throat dry. He leaned over, resting on the shelf once he'd placed the cheese back, his face in between his clenched fists.

What kind of shit was this? Feeling bad for the woman who'd ruined his life—a woman he'd wished dead numerous times. He sucked in a breath. *No way.* No fucking way was he going to allow the sick feeling in his stomach to grow anymore. He closed his eyes, shoving his phone in his pocket just as the door to the freezer opened. Vaida stood in front of him, a surprised look on her face.

"There you—oh god," she said as she got a closer look at his expression. "Everything okay?"

He clenched his jaw. "Fine." He hurried past her, refusing to let her see him break down. She grabbed a bag of lettuce, turning to face him.

"You sure?"

"Positive," he said, a bit too sharply. He tried to force a smile but he feared it looked more like he was going to throw up.

"Okay," she said, looking down. He turned away from her without another word and walked to Burt's office, knocking on the open door.

"I'm gonna cut out early," he said before Burt acknowledged him.

"Uh, you are? Why?" Burt asked, looking up and lowering his glasses.

"Family emergency," Fletcher said simply, feeling the unwelcome burn in his eyes once more.

"Jeez, I'm sorry, Fletch. Anything I can do?"

Fletcher made no move to wipe the tears he knew Burt must see. "Nope." He sniffed.

"Okay, Bud, sure. Go home, do whatever you need to."

Fletcher nodded, rubbing his cheek with his sleeve. "Thanks." He began to walk away but stopped, turning back around. "Can I get the next two days off too?"

Burt rolled his chair over to the wall where the schedule was posted and stared at it. "Yeah," he said finally. "Of course you can. Why don't you just take the whole week off?"

"No," Fletcher said, shaking his head. "I can't afford that. Two days is more than enough."

"It's paid," Burt said quietly, his eyes soft. "Just take it."

"I can't let you—are you sure?" he asked, stopping his own protest.

"Man, yeah, I'm sure. Obviously you need it. You've been doing a lot for this place lately. It's the least I can do for you." He wagged an ink pen at him. "I take notice of these things, you know. Just don't mention it to the others, okay?"

Fletcher nodded, patting the door. "Thank you."

Burt rolled back to his desk, looking down without

another word, and Fletcher walked out of the back and headed to the register to clock out.

"You leaving?" Aidan asked over the noise of the grill.

"Yeah, gotta run," Fletcher answered casually.

"Are you sure everything's okay?" Vaida asked, appearing behind him.

He nodded. "I'm going home for a bit. Family emergency. I'm sorry, but I'm gonna have to cancel our date tonight. I'll make it up to you when I get back."

"Yeah, of course," she said, nodding quickly. "I'm so sorry, Fletcher." She reached out, touching his arm carefully. "Is there anything I can do?"

"I'll be fine. I've just got to take care of a few things." He turned away from her, pretending to move the napkins from the counter when he felt himself getting choked up.

She walked in front of him, staring at him with knowing eyes. "Okay, well, be careful. I'll see you when you get back, right?"

He nodded, unable to speak, and hurried out of the diner.

SEVEN

VAIDA

Vaida entered Burt's office cautiously, staring at him until he looked up.

"Yeah?" he asked when he saw her.

"Sorry to bother you. Is everything okay with Fletcher?"

Burt leaned back in his chair. "You two close or something?"

"Sort of," she said, feeling silly. Were they really? "I want to be sure he's okay."

"He didn't say much," Burt told her. "Should I be worried?"

Vaida tucked a piece of hair behind her ear. "I don't know. I guess not." Her shoulders slumped, realizing how dumb she must sound. "Never mind," she said, starting to walk away.

"Vaida—" he called, standing up from his chair. She stopped, spinning back around.

"Yeah?"

"Do you know much about him? Fletcher?"

She shook her head. "Hardly anything."

"He's a good kid," he said, scratching his scalp. "Honestly, he is. But, he's quiet. Keeps to himself a lot. It makes me worry sometimes." She stared at him, not sure what to say. Truth was, she worried about Fletcher too, but what gave her the right to say that? She barely knew him. "I guess what I'm trying to say is that I want him to be okay. Maybe I should go after him? He said something about a family emergency, but as far as I knew he doesn't have family."

She pursed her lips. "I'd feel better if you did. It's maybe not my place but he seemed really upset. From what he's said to me, I don't think he has many people to help him through stuff like this." Whatever *this* might be.

"I don't think so either. It's good the two of you are close. I'll head out there now," Burt agreed. "Just to do a real quick check on him. Let me finish up a few things, and then I'll see if I can track down his address in his paperwork. Thanks for coming to me with this, Vaida."

"He lives downtown on Poplar," she told him.

He shook his head without looking up. "No, I don't think so."

"I'm pretty sure he does. He told me he lived across the street from a pizza place we met at. I'm sure that was the name of the street," she insisted.

He looked up, then down, flipping through a filing cabinet and pulling out a folder. He turned a few pages, running his finger across the form. "No, that's not the address I've got on file."

She took a breath. Had he lied to her? "Oh, maybe I was wrong then."

"I probably shouldn't do this," Burt said, pushing up his glasses. "But, if I give you the address, would you go there and check on him? If you are friends, I mean, it might be better for him to talk to you rather than me."

"I don't know if we're friends, really."

"You're the only one in my office asking about him," he said.

She nodded. "That's true. I'm happy to do it, but I don't get off until three."

He rolled his chair across the floor, glancing at the schedule. "Aidan and Marcus are here. If I have to, I'll call Jaxon in early. Fletcher's done a lot for me and this diner. What kind of shit boss would I be if I didn't at least check on him when he's down?"

She took the paper he held out, staring at the address. "Thanks, Burt."

He smiled. "Let me know that he's okay, all right?" She nodded. "Oh, and don't let Cody find out I'm not as much of a hardass as I like to put on, okay?"

"Deal."

WHEN VAIDA PULLED up to the address of the slip of paper, she gasped. It was a homeless shelter. She slowed down near the curb, putting the car in park and climbing out. She placed four quarters into the meter, keeping an eye on her surroundings. Her body was on edge, her mind racing.

Two men approached her and her pulse sped up. She

averted eye contact, hurrying past them and toward the door. This suddenly seemed like an awful idea. A woman called out to her, scratching nervously on her thin arms. "Hey," she said. Her thick eyeliner was smeared around her eyes. "Ain't seen you before."

"I'm looking for a friend of mine," Vaida said cautiously, keeping her distance from her. She couldn't help noticing how the woman's eyes traveled to her pocket where her phone was slightly sticking out. She put her arm down over it, feeling stupid. She knew enough not to bring her purse most anywhere in the city, but her phone never left her side.

"Friend? Who's that?" another man's voice asked from behind her. She jumped, turning around quickly. He was closer than she expected, his rotten breath on her face. She shuddered, backing up.

"His name's Fletcher Denali."

"Fletcher, hm?" the man growled.

"Do you know him?" she asked.

"What if we do? What's a pretty little thing like you gonna do for us if we help you out?" the man asked, taking a step toward her. She stepped back again, bumping into the woman, her thin body like a brick wall.

"Oh," Vaida squealed, ducking away from the couple. They circled her with greed in their eyes. Her breathing grew quick, feeling completely helpless. She looked to her car, trying to decide if she could make a break for it.

"He asked you a question," the girl snarled.

"I, um, I—" She reached for the keys she'd shoved in her back pocket, her throat growing dry as she tried to think quickly. The man made a sudden lunge for her and she screamed, throwing an arm up over her head to stop him.

"*Vaida*?" his voice rang out over them, and everyone froze.

"Fletcher?" she asked with a loud sigh, cold chills lining her arms. He shoved past the couple, rushing to her side.

"What the hell are you doing here?" He pulled her away from them and toward the street in a rush. "It's not safe for you to be here."

"What are *you* doing here, then?" she asked, keeping her head down as he forced her into the car and hurried around to the passenger's side.

"Lock the doors," he instructed as he shut his. "Now." She did as she was told, trying to calm her breathing. "How did you find me?"

"This is the address Burt has on file for you. We were worried about you after you'd left. He asked me to come check on you." She left out the part about it being her idea.

"You shouldn't have come," he said firmly.

"I didn't know what this place was until I was already here. What on earth are you doing here, anyway?"

Fletcher looked up, watching the man and woman who stood on the sidewalk, their eyes still locked on Vaida. "We need to get out of here."

"I couldn't agree more," she said, putting the car in drive and pulling out onto the surprisingly quiet street. "Now answer me, Fletcher. What were you doing at a place like that? Do you live there?"

He sighed, scratching his head. "Turn here."

"You told me you lived with Jaxon," she said, turning as he instructed.

"He lets me crash with him," he said as he pointed to another street. "Turn up here."

"So, are you going to tell me why you were living in a homeless shelter in the first place? And why you went back there today?"

"Are you going to tell me why it's any of your business?" he asked, his tone sharp.

She winced at his words. "It's not. I'm sorry, Fletcher. You're right. None of this is my business."

"I'm sorry," he apologized. "I didn't mean to snap. I just...I hate that you saw me there. I don't want you to think of me...*there*."

"I don't care where you live, Fletcher. I'm not interested in you because of the things you have. But, I do care that you're safe. And that you don't lie to me."

"I didn't lie. I don't live there anymore. I'm at Jaxon's most nights, like I told you." He paused. "And anyway, did you just admit you are interested in me?"

She rolled her eyes. "Don't change the subject."

He rubbed his knee, scratching at a speck of grease on his jeans. "It was temporary."

"How temporary? How long did you live there?" she asked.

"I don't know," he said, staring out the window. "Like I said, I crash with Jaxon most nights anyway. I did lie about having a bedroom, but only because I didn't want to seem so pathetic. It's just a one bedroom, but I can usually crash on the couch. I go back to the shelter for the night when he has a date, but Jaxon's place is where all my stuff is. What stuff I do have. I just haven't updated my address with Burt. Please don't tell anyone. I'm not ashamed, I did what I had to do to get by. But, I don't want anyone's pity." He looked at her. "Yours included."

She was filled with confusion, glancing over at him. "But, I don't understand. You work *so* much. I know we aren't making a fortune at the diner by any means, but you should be fine. Why would you need to stay in a shelter? Why would you even need to crash with Jaxon? You should have enough to afford somewhere permanent to live."

"Because all my money goes to taking care of my sister," he blurted out, his cheeks suddenly red.

"Your sister? The one who's sick? Is that the same one who killed your fiancée?" she asked. When he didn't answer, she took his silence as a *yes*. "Why would you help her? Does she know what it's costing you?"

"She doesn't need to know. I know this probably doesn't make any sense to you," he said. "My sister and I...we had a rough childhood. She's in psychiatric care because of it. What she did...it was awful, Vaida. And I hate her for it. But, I can't blame her entirely. She's still my sister."

"And you pay for all of her care? That's too much," she said wearily.

"There's no one else to foot the bill. Honestly, it's fine. I just don't want you to think any less of me."

"*Less?* Are you kidding me? I think you're amazing, Fletcher." She paused. "But, I also think you've got the weight of the world on your shoulders. That must be awful for you."

He looked away. "It's not so bad. Trust me, this is probably the most stable my life's ever been."

"Why were you at the shelter anyway? Today, I mean. You aren't going back there, are you?"

"No, I'm not going back," he told her, grimacing.

"What?" she asked.

"Well, the problem is, I actually want to date you. But, the more you know about me, the less desirable I become, I'm sure. So, here I go adding to the ever growing list of reasons why you should run far away from me, but...I don't have a car. I sold it to pay for a few months of my sister's treatments before I found work. I was at the shelter because I was asking a friend if I could borrow theirs."

"Your homeless friend has a car?" she asked skeptically.

"Some of them do," he told her. "But, this friend is a girl who worked there."

"So, did you find one to borrow, then?" She tried to ignore the instant, unfounded sting of jealousy that filled her chest. Why should she care that he went to another woman for help before coming to her? They barely knew each other. She had no claim over Fletcher, she reminded herself.

He shook his head. "She wasn't there."

"What do you need it for anyway?" He took a deep breath, reaching up and turning off the air conditioner with a shiver. "Fletcher?" she asked again.

"My mom died. I need to get home for the funeral."

"Oh. I'm so sorry," she told him.

"Don't be," he said, his lips tight. She turned down the next street, wanting to get away from downtown.

"What will you do?"

He closed his eyes. "I haven't figured it out. I'm probably going to have to call my brother to come get me."

"You don't seem like you think that's a good option," she said, reading his expression from her peripheral.

He shook his head. "Turn here." He pointed to a road on her left. "Who knows, I may not go at all. She doesn't deserve for anyone to be there."

She pressed her lips together at his harsh words, thinking quickly. "I could let you take my car."

"*No*," he said, as if that were the most preposterous thing he'd ever heard. "Thank you, but I'll figure something else out. I'm not leaving you in the city with no car."

"*You* live in the city with no car," she pointed out.

"I don't care about me. I'm not doing it to you. What if there's an emergency and you need the car? No way. It's really nice of you to offer, but I just can't. Trust me, she's not worth that."

She thought for a moment, worried her next suggestion might scare him off. "Well, then, I could go with you."

He turned his head, staring at her. "What?"

"I mean, if Burt would let me. He's worried about you, too. I'm sure if he knew the circumstances, he'd let me go. You could convince him."

"Why would you want to come with me?"

"Because," she said firmly. "Because, for whatever reason I can't explain, I care about you, Fletcher. I can't let you miss your mother's funeral if there's something I can do to prevent it."

He nodded, surprising her by not teasing her over what she'd said. "Are you sure?" he asked eventually. "My family is...well, we aren't the closest."

"Dark pasts and secrets, right?" she asked with a smirk. "Besides, a normal family might be enough to scare me away. I fit in perfectly with all things odd."

"Okay," he said. "Let's go back to your place then, and you can get your bag ready. I'll call Burt and work out the schedule." She bit her lip, hesitating, and it didn't go unnoticed by Fletcher. "Wait a second, you're going to roadtrip with me, but you don't trust me enough to know where you live?"

She sighed. "I do trust you. It's just...I have a hard time trusting anyone."

"I can understand that." He ran his tongue across his teeth, thinking. "I'll tell you what. Drop me off at Jaxon's, so I can run in and get a few things. You can go home and pack and then come back to get me when you're done."

She nodded, feeling relieved. "Okay."

EIGHT

VAIDA

When Vaida made it back to her apartment, she knocked on Cody's bedroom door cautiously. Truth be told, she wasn't sure what he did all day while she was at work.

He was a bartender at night, so she usually had the apartment to herself after she was off, but during the day he seemed to keep to himself, except for occasionally binge-watching a show with her. She couldn't complain. Cody was the closest thing she'd had to a friend since high school.

Until Fletcher. What was it about Fletcher that made her feel safe? She shook her head, ridding the thoughts from her mind before they started. She cared about him, but she would keep him at arm's length. Same with Cody. Same with everyone in her life. No one could ever know the truth about her.

She knocked again. The sound of her fist hitting the wood interrupted a groggy 'come in.' She pushed the door open at his words and waved to him. Cody lay in bed, the blanket wrapped around him like a burrito. His black hair stood in every direction, and he wiped his chin with his one free arm, sitting up sleepily. "Yeah?" he asked, staring at her.

"I didn't mean to wake you. I just wanted to let you know I'm going out of town for a day or two."

"Going out of town?" He stared at her, rubbing his eyes and blinking heavily, pulling the covers away from him. He grabbed his glasses from the side table, placing them over his nose.

"Yeah, I'm going away with Fletcher."

"Going to *Bonetown*, you mean?" He laid back on his pillows with his hands behind his head.

"His mother died. I'm taking him back home to her funeral," she said matter-of-factly.

"Taking him?" He winked. "He *needs* you?"

"Actually, yeah. He doesn't have a car."

He sat up instantly, looking appalled. "Mhm, honey, no. No, no, no. You can't be dating no *scrub*."

"He is not a scrub," she said, curling her lip. "Who even says that anymore?"

"Honey, the boy ain't got no car," he said, overpronouncing his words.

"Whatever," she said, feeling protective of Fletcher's secret. "I just wanted you to know so you wouldn't...I don't know...*whatever*."

"Worry?" he asked with one thick brow raised.

"Yeah." She looked down, feeling embarrassed. Who said he'd worry about her anyway? "Not that you would, but yeah."

"Too late. I'm already worried about you," he said with a

grin. "'Cause this boy's about to drain you of all your assets. And, baby, you ain't got no assets to be drained."

"I'll be fine, Cody," she said with a groan.

He smiled. "Seriously, though, be careful, okay?" When she nodded, he went on. "At what point during this little kidnapping excursion should I call a search party?"

"Give me three days," she said, only half-joking. "I'll keep in touch."

"Deal," he said, falling back onto the bed. "Now, let me go back to sleep." He pulled the pillow over his face dramatically. As she shut the door, she could hear him channeling his inner TLC with an obnoxious rendition of "No Scrubs."

NINE

FLETCHER

Fletcher left a scribbled note for Jaxon and grabbed his bag as he saw the small blue car pull up outside of the building. He frowned, looking at how rough he looked in the mirror. What was it about him that Vaida seemed to find so appealing? She was completely put together compared to him. There was a time, back in highschool, when he'd been confident in his looks. Before he'd let his muscles lose their bulge and his tan fade away. Now, all he could see when he looked at himself was the messy hair he kept dyed so dark it washed his skin tone out and the beard he'd given up on trying to keep neat. He'd once been popular, handsome, and comfortable around women, but those days seemed like distant memories. So much had changed in him since then.

He turned away, silencing the self-deprecating thoughts, and walked out the door, turning the key in the lock quickly. He walked downstairs, his footsteps echoing in the quiet stairwell, and passed through the glass doors that led to the street. She popped the trunk open as he approached her car, and he threw his bag next to hers before climbing into the passenger's seat.

"Ready to go?" she asked. "Before we do, is Burt okay with this? You called him, right? I can't afford to lose this job."

He nodded. "You're fine. We're both going to be pulling some extra shifts next week, but you're fine."

"I figured," she said with relief. "Apparently, he kind of likes you. Weird, right?"

He smiled at her. "Super weird."

"So, where are we headed?" She patted the wheel with her fingers.

"South." He pointed toward the interstate as she pulled out into the street. "My hometown is about three hours from here. A town called Dale." She lowered her brow, turning to look at him suddenly. "Is that too far? I'm sorry, I should've told you. I'll pay for gas, of course, but if it's too far I'll—"

"Dale?" she asked, her voice shaking.

"Yeah, why?"

She stopped the car abruptly, cars behind them honking and swerving to pass. "*Who are you?*" she demanded, her eyes wild.

Her eyes began searching around the car, her breath quick. "He sent you, didn't he?"

"He? He who? Vaida, we're in the middle of the road, we need to move before someone hits us." Panic was filling him the longer they sat still.

"Don't play dumb with me, Fletcher." Her voice was full of venom, and she seemed to not notice the traffic jam they were causing. "Where is he? Is he here?" She looked behind them. "How did he find me? How did *you* find me?" she asked through gritted teeth.

He reached for her hand, trying to calm her, but she jerked away. "Vaida, I honestly have no idea what you're talking about. I didn't *find* you. You came to work at the diner where I have been working for months. What on earth is going on?"

She was shaking, her eyes still searching around them as if she expected someone to jump out at any minute. It was obvious she was terrified, though Fletcher couldn't understand why. "Vaida, what's going on? Please talk to me. Who is 'he'?"

She crossed her arms. "There's no way you just happen to be from Dale. There's no way. I can't believe I trusted you. I can't believe I *liked* you. God, I'm so stupid." She pressed her head into the steering wheel, tears suddenly on her cheeks.

"Vaida, I'm not lying to you," he said softly. "I'll get out of this car right now if you want me to. I'll find another way home. You've been so kind to me already. I'm sorry I've scared you." He put his hand on the handle, ready to get out, when he heard a sniffle. He glanced her way. "Are you okay?" She didn't respond, staring straight ahead. "Look, if you could just maybe pull over to the shoulder? I don't want your car to get hit." Still, she said nothing. "Just, at least tell me you're okay. Are you in danger? You're really scaring me."

She let out a startling laugh.

"What's funny?" he asked.

"*I'm* scaring *you?*" She laughed again.

"I'm so fucking confused right now," Fletcher said. "What is happening?"

"I grew up in a town called Dakota, Fletcher," Vaida confessed. "It's—" A car behind them blared the horn, causing them both to jump, and Vaida put the car in drive again, moving slowly.

"It's an hour and a half from Dale. I know the town," Fletcher told her.

"Yeah, well, let's just say I have enemies there." She gave him a bitter smile.

"Enemies?"

"I really can't talk about it," she said, glancing in the rearview as she switched lanes. She looked over at him, her eyes studying his for a moment. "I shouldn't trust you."

"Vaida, I don't know what's going on, but I would never do anything to hurt you," he told her, begging her to believe him. "I care about you too much."

Her lip quivered. "Please don't make me regret this, Fletcher."

"Never," he promised. "I'm sorry about whatever is scaring you so much. I understand if you can't tell me, but just know that I will do everything I can to keep you safe. My promises mean something, Vaida. I don't make them lightly." She nodded without another word, and suddenly the car began to pick up speed. "Thank you for trusting me," Fletcher said after a moment, "because I'm trusting you, too."

"Trusting me how?" she asked, still not looking at him.

He spoke softly, never having had to speak his secret out loud before. "Because I'm about to tell you the biggest secret I have. One that could ruin my life." He looked at her, watching her expression. "My name isn't Fletcher."

She slammed on the brakes again, this time pulling over onto the shoulder quickly. He grabbed the handle above his head to prevent his head from slamming into the window. This girl was going to kill him. "What does that mean?" she demanded.

"My name is Gavin James," he said, staring into her eyes with a sick feeling in his belly. "And for all intents and purposes, I'm dead."

TEN

FLETCHER/GAVIN

As he said the words, an odd mixture of fear and relief filled his chest. Her eyes were stone cold as she glared at him.

"What do you mean you're dead?" she asked with no power behind her voice.

"My sister and I escaped a very abusive home when we were seventeen. Our parents were...just awful. Drunk and abusive, neglectful, same old story you've heard a thousand times."

"I'm so—" she started, staring at him in horror.

"Please, you don't need to be sorry. It was a long time ago. Anyway, the only way we could escape was to fake our own deaths. We started a fire, and as far as anyone knows, we died in that fire." He was shaking now, adrenaline coursing through him. "Us and my father. My father actually did die, though, but we got out."

"Oh my god," she gasped.

"So, you see, if anyone were to find out the truth about me, about who I am...I would go to jail. My sister, too. So, now, you hold all the power."

She nodded. "Why would you tell me that?"

"Because I trust you. And because I need you to trust me."

"SO, aren't you worried about going back home? I mean, you could be caught," Vaida said after half an hour of driving.

"The only person who knows what I look like now is my brother, well, him and my sister-in-law. No one is looking for me. Besides, I don't think many people will make it to my mother's funeral. She wasn't exactly a Georgia peach."

Vaida frowned, feeling a lump in her throat. "Why do you want to go?"

"Huh?"

"You said it yourself, she's awful. Why would you want to go?"

"She's still my mom, Vaida," he said stiffly.

"I didn't mean—"

"Besides, it makes me feel better knowing she's actually gone. I'm finally safe. I need to see her to believe it."

She nodded. "I'm glad you're safe."

He reached out his hand for hers, but she remained still. "What about your sister? Have you told her? Will she be able to come?"

"No," he said, "no. I can't take her out of her clinic. Besides, she can't go back around my brother. She's dangerous. He'd never accept it."

“Your brother hates her? Why? She killed your fiancée, and you don’t even hate her.”

He groaned. “Yeah, well, she tried to kill his wife and daughter.”

She gasped, gripping the steering wheel firmly. “Oh my god. Why?”

He frowned, looking out the window. "She's in a bad place, Vaida. It's no excuse, and most days you’re wrong, I *do* hate her for what she's done. But I can't ignore her. I'm all she's got in the world. If I turn my back on her, she's done for. She'll never survive without me."

She was silent.

"I don't expect you to understand. Gunner sure doesn't. I'll never forgive her because it would be a betrayal to the woman I loved more than anything in the world. But, Fiona is more than just my sister. She's my twin. We've been together literally since the moment we began to exist. Some part of me will always want to protect her."

"I'm sorry, Gavin," she said in a whisper. "I had no idea."

"No one does. It's my burden to bear."

"You don’t talk about your fiancée much,” she said, a question in her statement.

"Her name was Holly."

She turned on her blinker, switching lanes. "Tell me about her."

"We met in high school. She was nothing I was looking for but absolutely everything I needed. My sister was working on a project with her for some class in school. I came with her to Holly’s house one night. I just...I loved her from the moment I met her. That sounds cheesy, I know, but it’s the truth. She was funny and smart and completely unafraid of anything. Before I left Dale, we were partners in crime. Our adventures changed my life. When I died, well...you know—" He put air quotes around the word 'died.' "She was devastated. But I was...distraught. It was the worst part of my life. She was the one I missed. So, eventually I contacted her. She ran away with us. My sister Fiona, her name's really *Gia,* hated me. She never trusted her with our secret. But, it was my decision." He wiped a tear from his eyes quickly. "She got pregnant and Gia lost her mind. It's my fault Holly's dead...because I loved her too much to let her go."

Vaida's eyes were full of horror. "Flet—*Gavin,* I don't know what to call you anymore."

"You can call me either one." He shrugged, looking out the window to his right.

"You can't blame yourself."

"But, I do. I always will. If I'd left her alone, let her believe I was gone like I should have, she would've been safe. She would be settled down with a family. Kids, probably, and some normal husband with a job at a bank or something. Safe and alive. Because of me, she's gone. Because of me, she'll never get to have anything ever again." He took a sharp breath, turning away so she wouldn't see the tears that filled his eyes once more. He'd never been able to talk about Holly. No one was there to listen. It was the first time he'd allowed himself to admit his darkest thoughts to anyone.

She reached her hand out, squeezing his. "Because of you, she lived. From what you've said, she filled your life with incredible joy. Don't you believe you did the same for her?" When he didn't answer, she went on. "If she didn't feel the same, she wouldn't have come with you. It's not your fault she died, Gavin. That's on your sister. It *is* your fault she had happiness and love. That's what you get to take credit for. Trust me, there are horrible men out there. Men who deserve blame for horrible things. You—" She took a breath. "You are not one of those men."

He ran a thumb along her knuckles. "You're amazing, you know that?"

"Far from it," she said softly.

"Vaida, since Holly, no one has ever made me feel the way you do."

She looked at him. "And what way is that?"

"Like not everything in my life has to be bad."

She squeezed his hand, their skin warm against each other's. "You deserve good in your life. Of all people, you do. But, I don't think I'll be it."

"Why's that?"

She shook her head. "I'm not good for anyone." She smiled sadly. "Too much baggage."

"Are you kidding me? Have you been listening to all the baggage I come with?"

She laughed. "Mine makes yours look like carry-on."

He rubbed her hand with his free hand. "See, it's like I told you, we're a perfect match."

ELEVEN

GAVIN

They arrived in Dale after dark and Gavin directed her to the only operating motel left in the tiny, desolate town.

"It's not much," he said cautiously. "Dakota probably has better places to stay if you want to go there."

"No," she answered quickly. "Here is fine."

She didn't want to go back to Dakota, because of who she'd called her *enemies,* he assumed. Gavin was curious about them, but he refused to pry. When, if, she decided it was his business, she would tell him. He climbed out of the car, grabbing their bags from the trunk. "Do you...want separate rooms? Or...?" he trailed off.

"I don't mind bunking together. As long as you don't get any crazy ideas."

He winked. "Why, I'd never, Miss Vaida. I'm a gentleman to my very core." They walked into the small lobby, his hand around her waist. "We need a room, please."

The man at the counter's name was Dennis. He recognized him instantly as the soft-spoken man who had once run the small grocery store on the corner. The motel had been run by a different family all those years ago, one Gavin couldn't recall the name of. Dennis eyed Gavin as though he might recognize him but didn't comment on it. Gavin felt fear growing in him but tried to remain calm.

"Just one?"

"Just one," he responded, looking down.

The man typed something into the computer, reciting the rate to him and accepting the cash he held out. "We need a card to keep on file." Gavin hesitated, reaching into his back pocket with a racing heart. He pulled out the only credit card he owned with his fake name on it. The only credit card he owned, period. He watched the man read his name, raising his eyebrows and swiping the card. "Room fifteen," he told them, handing over a room key and the credit card.

Gavin turned quickly, leading Vaida back outside and to their room. He pushed open the heavy door, letting her walk in first. The room smelled of stale cigarettes and looked as though it's last makeover had been in the late seventies. He let out a sigh of relief at seeing they'd been given two queen beds. "Which bed do you want?" he asked, setting their bags on the small desk beside the large, box television.

"This one's fine," she said, sitting down on the maroon comforter and pulling her shoes off. "I'm exhausted."

"Thank you for coming with me, Vaida," he said, pulling his own shoes off.

She looked up at him, surprise in her eyes. "You're welcome."

"I wish we could be somewhere better than this for our first trip together."

She shook her head. "First trip, hm? Do you plan on taking more?"

He smiled, rubbing his head. "I hope so."

She stood up. "This place isn't so bad. It has a sort of charm to it, don't you think?"

"Yeah," he agreed. "Between the amazing view of the parking lot—" He gestured to the window. "And the cigarette burns on the carpet, this is a regular haven."

She laughed. "Well, lucky for you, I'm not a caviar and mints on my pillow kind of girl."

He walked to his bag, grabbing a pair of basketball shorts and a t-shirt from it. "Well, lucky me."

TWELVE

GAVIN

The next morning, Gavin woke up before Vaida. He walked out of the hotel room, careful not to wake her and dialed Gunner's number.

"Hello?" Gunner asked.

"Hey, it's me."

"Hey, what's up?"

"I'm home."

"Home? You're in Dale? I thought you weren't coming."

"Yeah, well...I didn't think I was either. What time's the service?"

"Oh, man. I'm so glad you decided to come. It's at eleven. Reagan and I will be headed that way soon," Gunner said. Gavin could hear one of the kids crying in the background.

"Okay," he said. "We'll be there."

"We?" Gunner asked defensively.

"Yeah, um, I'm bringing someone with me."

"Who?" he asked. "Not *her*?"

"No," Gavin answered. "Her name's Vaida. She's..." he stopped. He didn't know what to tell him, didn't know what they were. "I really like her, man."

"Does she know the truth about you?"

"Yeah, actually she does."

Gunner paused. "I'm really happy for you."

"She'll never replace Holly," Gavin told him, as if he needed to justify that.

"I know."

"I'll see you soon, brother," Gavin said finally.

"See you soon."

He pressed a finger onto the screen, ending the call, and walked back into the motel room. Vaida sat up in bed, yawning. "Good morning," she told him, her voice throaty. He smirked at her, his heart jumping at the sight of her.

"Sleep good?" he asked.

"Like a baby," she told him. "Which is actually rare for me. I think I feel safe when you're around."

He stared at her, something catching in his throat. Her voice was vulnerable. "Well, then, I guess you need to have me around more often."

She nodded. "Maybe so."

He walked to her bed, sitting down in front of her. "The service is at eleven. If you want, I can run out and grab us some breakfast while you get ready."

She frowned. "I'd rather you didn't leave."

"Okay," he said quickly. "That's fine, too. How about we get ready, and then we can grab breakfast on our way?"

"Sounds good," she said, running a hand through her disheveled hair. "Can I shower first?"

"Be my guest," he said, holding a hand out. She stood from the bed, hurrying past him in her pajama shorts and tank top. He couldn't stop his eyes from wandering but looked away quickly. She pulled a small bag and a handful of clothes from her larger bag and disappeared into the bathroom.

As she shut the door, Gavin walked to his own bag, digging through it to find his black dress shirt and slacks. He didn't own a suit, and there was no way he was going to spend his money on one just for Misty. This would have to do. He ran a comb through his hair, brushing his teeth at the small sink outside of the bathroom. He wet the comb, brushing over his dark hair and beard until they'd been tamed. He pulled his shorts off, changing boxers quickly and pulling on his slacks. Next came his shirt, he ran a hand over his scarred chest, knowing his back looked worse.

When he was young, his tan had concealed the silver scars from his father's belt and the purple circles from the cigarettes his mother had lived off of, but as he'd grown older, his now pale skin illuminated the marks that had haunted his childhood. He ran a finger across the worst of it, a thin red scar from his side to his lower belly, where Misty had cut him with glass from a picture frame he'd bumped into when he was seven. He could still remember the ice cold fear that filled him when she'd seen his mess.

He heard Vaida shutting the shower off and pulled his shirt on quickly. No one besides Gunner, Holly, and Gia had ever seen his scars, and he wasn't sure he'd ever be comfortable enough to let anyone else see them. He was buttoning his shirt when the bathroom door opened, a cloud of steam billowing out. She was standing in the middle of the tiny bathroom, a white towel wrapped around her thin frame. She wore a black shower cap over her hair, and he couldn't help but grin.

She narrowed her eyes at him. "What's so funny?"

"Nice shower cap, granny," he joked.

"Do you know how long it takes me to fix my hair?" she asked. "We would be here all day if I had to wash and style it."

"I'm not judging," he said. "It's cute."

She shook her head, walking out to stand beside him. She set her bag on the counter, grabbing out a few packages of makeup and her toothbrush. She brushed her teeth as he walked back to his bag and put his clothes away. When he returned, she had begun applying her makeup. He was surprised to see she looked so much like herself without makeup on. She didn't wear much. She took a bottle of a dark liquid, placing a purple sponge to it. She blotted her face, light circles blending into her warm skin. She stopped, staring at him. "Are you going to watch me the whole time?"

He blushed. "I like watching you."

She furrowed her brow. "That's not creepy at all."

He finished buttoning his shirt, shaking his head. "Should I look away?"

She didn't answer, moving on to run a pencil-like brush over her brows. She applied black liquid to her lids and ran a coat of what he thought was called mascara over her dark lashes. Last, she pulled a tube of brown lipstick out, running it over her lips slowly. Her eyes flirted with his as she pushed her lips out. When she was finished, she reached up, pulling her shower cap off so that her thick, black hair fell past her shoulders. She grabbed a comb from her bag, running it through her hair. The light gleamed off of it. She reached into her bag, pulled out a green container, and ran her hands through the putty. It smelled of coconuts as she rubbed the cream in.

It took all of his willpower not to pull her to him and run his own hands through her hair, breathing in her scent. Seeming to know exactly what he was thinking, she pulled her gaze from his, turning and walking back into the bathroom. She shut the door behind her and he exhaled, not realizing he'd been holding his breath. He could hear her moving around in the bathroom, and he forced himself to walk away, though he desperately wanted to stay close to her.

When she appeared again, she had slid on a thin black dress that hung off her curves. She walked to her bag, placing her dirty clothes into a separate plastic bag and shoving it out of sight. She grabbed a pair of heels and slid them on before turning back to face him. She sighed. "Look okay?"

He nodded. "You look amazing, Vaida," he told her, and she shoved him playfully, looking down as if she were self-conscious.

"It's an old dress."

"Well, you look amazing in a grease covered t-shirt at work, so I don't know why you're surprised."

She shook her head, pressing her lips into a small smile. "You don't look so bad yourself."

"I know," he told her, a sly grin on his face. He held his arm out. "Now, I'm starving. Ready to go eat?"

She placed her arm through his. "Lead the way."

THIRTEEN

GAVIN

When they arrived at the gravesite, Gavin saw Gunner and Reagan immediately. Nora and their new baby, Duncan, weren't with them. Gavin climbed out of the car, walking around to open the door for Vaida, but she was one step ahead of him. She pushed the door open, stepping out and taking his hand when he held it out to her.

Gunner and Reagan approached them, looking solemn. It was an odd feeling, the place in his chest where grief should have been was filled with only relief.

"Fletcher," Gunner said, reaching up to hug his brother.

"You can call me Gavin," Gavin told him, squeezing his shoulders. "She knows everything." Gunner pulled away, holding a hand out to shake Vaida's. "This is Vaida," Gavin introduced them to her. "Vaida, this is my brother, Gunner, and his wife, Reagan."

"It's nice to meet you both," she said, shaking their hands.

"We're glad you could come," Reagan told Gavin. "It means a lot to Gunner."

Gavin nodded. "I almost didn't. Where are the kids?"

"My parents are watching them," Reagan answered.

"There was no reason for them to be here," Gunner said. "They never knew Misty."

Gavin agreed. "They were better for it."

No one responded to his bitter comment. Instead, they turned, walking toward where the casket sat. "No pastor?" Gavin asked, staring around at the empty cemetery.

"No. It's not like Misty had ties to any faith. I just kept it simple. Especially since she had no life insurance."

"Do you need help with the cost?" Gavin asked, praying he'd say no.

"No." Gunner waved him off. "We're fine. I'm working at the port again. Besides, like I said, we went cheap."

"Still more than she deserved," Gavin said.

There was a blue tent set up where the funeral home worker sat. When they approached, he stood up. "Do you want me to say a few words?" he asked.

"No," Gunner said. "That's all right. We'll just be a minute."

He sat back down. "Take your time."

Gavin stared at the light brown casket that housed the woman who'd ruined his life. He was surprised to feel cool tears suddenly filling his vision. He sucked in a breath, pretending to scratch his eye to keep them away. If anyone noticed, they didn't react. No one touched the casket, though they all stared at it in horror. Vaida squeezed his hand tighter, his palm warm against his.

"Good-bye, Misty," Gunner whispered.

Good riddance, Gavin thought.

FOURTEEN

GAVIN

After the short service, Gunner invited Gavin and Vaida back to their house.

"You should've let us know you were in town last night," Reagan said. "You didn't need to stay in the motel. You know we have plenty of room."

"We didn't want to put you out. Besides, we got in sort of late."

"You're welcome anytime, Gav, you know that," Gunner told him.

Gavin nodded. He didn't feel welcome. Reagan and Gunner had been nothing short of amazing to him since he'd re-entered their lives, but still he couldn't forget their bumpy start. Things between the three of them would always feel strained. "Thanks."

As they climbed into Vaida's car, finally just the two of

them again, Gavin took a breath. "Are you sure this is okay? We don't have to go back with them if you're uncomfortable."

"I'm fine, Fl-Gavin," she said. She still confused his name occasionally. "Honestly. Your brother and sister-in-law are sweet. I don't mind."

"Okay," he said as she pulled out, following the silver SUV Gunner drove out of the cemetery.

"Are you okay?" she asked after a few moments.

"You know, it's the strangest feeling. I feel guilty that I don't feel bad," he said honestly. "The only thing I really feel is relief. Truth is, I blame Misty for everything bad in my life. Holly's death, especially. I blame her more than Gia. That's probably not healthy, right?"

She shrugged. "I'm certainly not a shrink. I think however you feel, you're entitled to feel that way. You can't change your emotions."

He nodded. "I mean, she was my mom, but she was never motherly. I never felt the way Gunner felt about her. As a kid, I never saw the side that he saw. I guess it was in there, somewhere, but I never got to experience that part of her. All I remember is how awful she was to me."

"You're allowed to feel however you do about her, Gavin. Just being your mother doesn't excuse her wrongs. If people wanted you to speak kindly of them, they should've been kinder," Vaida said. "That's something my grandma used to say."

Gavin smiled. "She sounds like a smart woman."

"She was amazing."

"Was?"

"She passed away when I was eighteen."

"I'm sorry, Vaida."

"Thank you," she said politely as they pulled into the small driveway in front of the yellow house. They climbed out of the car together, walking up the paved drive. Gavin was sure the house had once been blue.

"Come in," Reagan told them, unlocking the door and pushing it open so they could walk in first. "You'll have to excuse the mess." Gavin looked around, unable to see what mess she could be talking about. For having two children, the house was nearly pristine. They stood awkwardly in the living room until the door shut. "Please, make yourselves at home," Reagan said. "Vaida, do you like tea? I can put some on."

"Um, sure," Vaida answered. "That'd be great."

Reagan hurried past them, and Gunner sat down, holding out his hands as if to say they should sit as well. "So, where did you two meet?"

"We work together," Gavin answered. "How are the kids?" He changed the subject quickly.

"They're great. Nora's growing like crazy and Duncan's starting to crawl and pull up to things. It's strange how fast it goes." Gavin spied a picture of the children on the table, both smiling with Gunner's bright grin and Reagan's green eyes. Occasionally, Gunner had sent him pictures and updates of the two, but Gavin had yet to meet their newest addition and his last encounter with Nora had been at the hospital after Gia had nearly killed her. He was sure the child wouldn't have the fondest of memories of him.

"That's good, Gun. I'm glad to see things are going well for you." He genuinely meant the sentiment, but he knew his words must've come out bitter.

Gunner got an uneasy look on his face. "Are things good with you? I mean, you're okay?"

"I'm okay," he said, nodding. "Nothing too exciting in my life. Well, besides her." He glanced toward Vaida, who scrunched her nose up shyly and looked down.

"Are you from Atlanta, Vaida?" Gunner asked, resting his chin on his knuckles, his elbow on the arm of the chair.

Vaida tensed beside him, but Gavin was sure Gunner hadn't noticed. "Yes, around there," she answered quickly.

Gunner nodded. After a few awkward minutes had passed, Reagan appeared with four mugs of steaming tea. "I didn't know how you would take yours, but we have sugar, honey or lemon," she said like a proper Southern woman. Truth was, Gavin had never had any tea besides iced and sweet, and he could sense that Vaida probably hadn't either.

"This is great, Reagan," he said, taking his mug. He wasn't a fan of hot drinks in general, as he hated to wait for anything to cool.

Gunner cleared his throat, leaning forward over his knees. "Gav, I have something I need to talk to you about."

"Okay, shoot."

Gunner looked to Reagan, who looked down, stirring her tea. Gavin instantly realized there was an ulterior motive to them being invited back to the house. Gunner had bad news; it was written all over his face. "I, um." He rubbed his mouth with his thumb, avoiding eye contact. His hands clasped together in front of him as he looked back up. "I don't want you to freak out because I'm handling it, but I think you should know what's going on."

"What are you talking about?"

He blew air through his nose, his eyes full of sorrow. "When Misty died, she left a note with her nurse."

"A note?"

"A letter," Gunner said.

"And what did the letter say?"

"She—" He paused, running his face through his open palm. "She wanted the police to know the truth about you and Gia. That you're still alive and...that you killed Dad."

He swallowed hard, his skin going cold. "What?"

"In the letter, she talked about how Gia started the fire and how you've both been in hiding since."

"Oh my god," Gavin spat, hatred filling him.

"I know," Gunner said. Reagan ran a hand over his arm, clutching him and looking at Gavin with worry. "Her dying wish was to make sure the two of you suffered." Gunner's jaw tightened with disdain. "She didn't know where you were hiding, thank god. And so, at this point, it's all just the ramblings of a deranged woman, but the cops seemed to be taking what she said seriously at first."

"What?" he asked, his pulse pounding.

"They've been here to question me. Yesterday after we talked. Reagan and I insisted she was insane. That the cancer had messed with her memory. I don't think you have anything to worry about. I think they believed our story, but I just wanted to warn you. I don't know what they're doing to check into it, but I want you to be careful."

"I shouldn't have come back," Gavin said. "Why wouldn't you tell me that before I came back? Do you have any idea how dangerous it is for me to be here?"

"I only found out about it yesterday, and from what you said on the phone, I didn't think you'd be coming. I didn't want to call you back to warn you not to come after I'd just spoken to the police. Just in case they are watching me or something. But, I don't think they are. Honestly, I don't think they're too worried about it. Enough time has passed, they'd be chasing their tails looking for you."

"You don't know that, Gunner."

"Even if they do find you, you have your story, your new ID. You *are* Fletcher Denali. They have no reason to believe you aren't. As far as anyone knows, Gavin died in that fire. And there's no one left to deny that. You know I'll protect you however I can."

Gavin nodded, not feeling any more reassured. "Do you think they'll come back?"

"I don't think so. I hope not." The room was silent, solemn looks on everyone's faces.

"Why would she do something so horrible? What did she have to gain from hurting you after she was already gone?" Vaida asked, touching Gavin's arm.

Everyone's eyes went to her, but no one seemed to have an answer. "That's just who she was," Gavin said eventually. "Evil and spiteful to her very core."

"Well, enough bad news," Reagan said. "Nothing good is going to come from dwelling on it now. Would you guys like to stay overnight? I can make up the guest room for you. We'd love to have you."

"Uh, no," Gavin said quickly. "We'll probably head back into the city tonight."

"Are you sure?" Gunner asked, though Gavin couldn't help noticing he looked slightly relieved.

"Yeah, I've got to get back to work, anyway. Thanks for the offer though."

"Sure, man, anytime. You're always welcome here."

Gavin took a sip of his still-too-hot tea, ignoring the burn.

"Would you at least stay for dinner, then?" Reagan asked. "It's nearly that time, and I know the kids would love to see you. My parents will be bringing them home soon."

"I don't know," he said, looking to Vaida.

"I don't mind," she offered.

He sighed, looking at Reagan's hopeful expression. At that moment, something in her eyes reminded him of Holly and he knew it would be impossible to say no. "Okay, yeah, that would be great."

"Yeah?" Gunner asked, a smile growing on his face.

"Yeah," Gavin said. "As long as you don't need to get back?" he asked Vaida.

"I go where you go," she promised, and he found himself hoping that would remain true.

FIFTEEN

GAVIN

Once they were in the car, Gavin apologized to Vaida. "I'm sorry. I know things with my brother are awkward. We have a complicated history, and neither of us have ever really made it past that."

"It wasn't awkward. They seemed sweet," she said. "At least they were trying."

"Yeah," he said. "They're good people. For the only family I've really got, I can't complain."

"We could have stayed, you know. If you wanted to. I'm in no rush to get back to work. They seemed to want to visit with you more."

"I know," he said, "but I just can't. It's like...when I'm around them, I can't breathe."

"What do you mean?"

"I can't explain it, it's just, I feel like I'm suffocating. Like I can't catch my breath until I'm away from them."

"Is it because of your past?"

He nodded. "I guess so. We've tried to move on from it, and we're better than we've been in years. But, I'm still not totally comfortable around them. I still feel like the family screw up."

She took a deep breath. "Ahh, I know that feeling all too well."

"No way," he said. "You couldn't possibly be a screw up."

"Ah, ah, ah," she said, wagging her finger. "But I can. And I am."

Gavin looked in the rearview, noticing a set of headlights that had been following them for a while, and his gut instantly told him something wasn't right. Working off a hunch, he turned on his blinker. Within seconds, the car turned on its blinker as well. Gavin's breathing hitched, fear turning to adrenaline. "Vaida, I don't want you to panic, but we're being followed."

"What?" she asked, turning around in her seat to look at the car behind them. "Who is it?"

"I don't know," he said. "We're okay, just stay calm." With that, he turned on the next street without a blinker, watching as the car did the same. His phone began buzzing inside his pocket. He reached in, grabbing it and pulling it out. The screen held a number he didn't recognize. His gaze fell on Vaida's fear-filled eyes, and he tried to smile as a means to keep her calm.

"Probably a wrong number," he explained. "Hello?"

"Gavin?" Gunner's hurried voice came over the speaker.

"Yeah?"

"You're being followed."

He glanced around, his heart bellowing in his chest. "Yeah, I know. How do you know that?"

"Right after you left, an officer came back to our house. He saw you at the service and then saw you come back to our house. I told him you're a cousin on Dad's side, but I don't know if he bought it. He asked where you were staying and said they wanted to talk to you, but I told him you were headed back to Charleston."

Gavin cursed under his breath. "Right, good."

"Gavin, I'm sorry I let you come back. I really didn't think you were in any danger. I should've done something more to protect you."

"It's okay," he said. "You didn't know. I'm going to get off here so I can lose this guy."

"Please check in when you can. This is Reagan's parents' phone. You can call back on it and they'll relay the message."

"Okay, take care of yourself, Gunner."

"You too, Gav," he said before the line clicked and his voice was gone.

"It's the police," Gavin told her. "They saw us at the service, and now they're asking questions about me. Look, Vaida, I don't want to get you in any trouble. Being associated with me, it's not a good idea. I'm so sorry I've gotten you mixed up in this mess."

"What are we going to do?" she asked.

He closed his eyes, trying to think. "I could turn myself in. That way you don't end up in any trouble. You don't have to admit you knew anything about who I am."

"Gavin, no. There's no reason for you to do that for me. They haven't even turned on their lights. They aren't trying to pull us over."

She was right, he knew, which made him even more confused. Why would they be merely following him? Maybe to determine where he lived, but would they really follow him all the way to Atlanta? Or to Charleston if they believed Gunner's story?

"I'm going to try and lose them," he said. "They're making me nervous following us like this."

She nodded, holding onto the door handle. "Okay, that's fine. I trust you."

He turned a sharp corner, increasing his speed. The car was right on his tail. He pressed the gas harder, the car behind him gaining speed. He turned right and then left, squeezing down an alley where he and Holly had once hid when they'd skipped school. He was lucky, having knowledge of the town on his side would only be an advantage, but then again, the cop would know the same parts of the town he did. It wasn't like Dale was big enough to disappear in.

Except he had. Once upon a time. He shook his head, seeing the headlights shining in his rearview again. "Hold on," he warned, turning down another alley and speeding up. He turned right, then left, then right again, speeding onto the highway. He cut off two cars, watching the mirror to see if he was still being followed.

"Did we lose them?" Vaida asked.

Gavin shook his head. "No way, it was too easy." The next road was a few feet ahead of them, but the cop's car never pulled out. He continued gaining speed, going over the limit through the small town. He turned down the gravel road as they reached it, pulling into the dirt path of the cornfield and shutting off the car. His lights went off in an instant and they sat, breathing heavily and watching in silence. The night around them was still as the tall corn blew in the wind. Beside him, Vaida shifted in her seat. Their breath had begun to fog up the window, and suddenly he saw a pair of headlights turn down the quiet street. "Shh," he whispered, though she wasn't making any noise.

They sat still, frozen in silence, Gavin's heart racing and his throat dry. The headlights crept down the road slowly, growing closer to them. The car passed them, moving at a snail's pace but never stopping. Once it was past, Gavin let out a loud breath. Relief washed over him, his heart still pounding in his ears. He looked to Vaida, whose eyes had small tears in them.

"Are you okay?" he asked.

She shook her head. "Gavin, I—" she stopped, her voice rife with tears.

"What is it?" he asked, leaning into her and taking her arms in his hands.

"I've put you in terrible danger."

"What are you talking about?"

"That cop car wasn't from Dale," she said. He nodded.

"Yeah, weird, right? It was a county cop."

She nodded. "I have something to tell you."

"What is it?"

"I don't think the cops are looking for you," she said plainly. "I think they're looking for me."

SIXTEEN

VAIDA
BEFORE

To be fair, Vaida had never meant for things to happen the way they did. After that night, she tried all forms of coping, including reasoning and bargaining, to convince herself that what she did was okay. If he hadn't come home early, she could've handled it better. If he hadn't felt guilty, he wouldn't have come home early. If she hadn't made him mad the night before, he wouldn't have anything to feel guilty about. If he hadn't beaten the shit out of her again, she might not have made him mad. If she'd been better prepared, none of it would've happened.

In the end, it always came back to her. Her fault, her fault, her fault. That was what years of emotional abuse did to a person. It was never going to be anyone's fault but her own. Just like it was her decision that caused the downward spiral that was now her life.

She ran through the house, soaked in the blood she would've once died to protect. Her heart pounded, fresh tears on her cheeks. She hurried into the bathroom, grabbing a towel and attempting to wipe away any evidence of what she'd done. She stripped out of her clothes, shaking so hard she was sure she would fall down, and scrubbed her arms under the running water of the sink. Her face was speckled with his blood. She rubbed her cheeks with her fingers, watching the blood as it mixed with the water and swirled down the drain. She should clean it with bleach, burn her clothes, and clean up her mess, but she didn't have time. Her stomach was churning, and her body burned with a need to get out of that house. She couldn't think straight, couldn't seem to catch her breath.

She hurried from the bathroom, grabbing a trash bag from the kitchen on her way through. His body lay on the floor, but she refused to look his way. She couldn't, for fear that she would totally lose it. She shoved her clothes and the gun into the bag, rushing toward the laundry room. She threw on a pair of sweatpants and a hoodie, pulling the hood up over her head and pushing her hair back. She didn't bother to grab her phone, but took her purse and the car keys as she rushed out the door.

She climbed in the car, looking around at the neighboring houses to see if her guilty getaway was being witnessed, but she saw noone. As she started the car up, she heaved a sigh of relief, the first real relief she'd felt in years. Even if she was caught—even if she was doomed to spend the rest of her life in jail—for the next few seconds, hours, and possibly days, she would be free. And that was the most hope she'd had in years.

SEVENTEEN

VAIDA
BEFORE

Later that day, Vaida walked into a rundown gas station just south of Atlanta. She was nearly out of money, and she didn't dare use her credit cards for anything in case they were already looking for her. She doubted that, his brother wouldn't be by until Sunday, so she should have at least two more days of freedom. But, she couldn't be sure. She couldn't be sure of anything, honestly.

"Can I get," she paused, digging through her wallet, "um, seven dollars in gas on pump two?" she asked, pulling out the wadded up dollar bills.

The attendant nodded. "Okay, sure."

She ducked her head, trying not to make eye contact with him. She needed to make sure no one would remember her. After a moment, the man handed her a receipt and she hurried out the door.

As she filled her tank, she looked around. She was so thirsty and had started to grow desperate for a shower, still feeling as though his blood was on her skin. She climbed in her car, opened her glovebox, and pulled out a hair tie. She pulled her hair back in a ponytail, rubbing the mascara from her eyes and grimacing. She knew what she had to do. She grabbed a pocket knife from her purse, pulling her long ponytail to the side and running the blade over the locks until there was hardly enough left to pull up. She tossed the wad of hair into a nearby trash can, feeling somewhat better.

She had less than thirty dollars left, no food or water, and nowhere to sleep but her car. Even with the thirty-miles-to-the-gallon her car got, she wouldn't be able to make it much further without more money. But stopping would mean exposing herself. She had planned to leave the state, head as far north as possible before they started to search for her, but she had no resources to support that plan. Not yet, anyway.

She pulled out of the gas station, heading into Atlanta's downtown. The traffic was steady and she was getting cut off at every turn, but her usual road rage couldn't be summoned in that moment. Every emotion she should've been feeling was numbed by one: complete determination to survive.

She pulled off on an exit before she reached the busy downtown, driving into a parking lot for the first bar she saw. After high school, she'd tended bar for a small local restaurant, and any bar was surely a place where she could remain inconspicuous for a few days until she could earn enough tip money to get her further away. If nothing else, at least maybe they'd take pity on her and offer her some water.

She stepped out of her car, not at all dressed for an interview, but what choice did she really have? When she entered the dark building, she locked eyes with the man behind the counter. He was thin and handsome with a strong jaw, striking grey eyes, and shiny black hair. He smiled at her.

"Hey, honey," he greeted her as she approached the bar. "What can I get for you?"

"Um, actually, I'm here about a job."

"A job?" he asked, raising a thick eyebrow.

"I wondered if you might have room for another bartender," she asked, not sounding entirely confident. "I could really use the work. I have experience, and it could just be temporary—"

"I'm sorry," he said, cutting her off. "We don't really have any openings right now. I can leave your name with my boss in case that changes."

Her face fell, though she tried to keep the small smile in place. "Oh, okay," she said politely. "Well, thank you anyway."

"What was your name?" he asked before she could turn away.

"Vaida," she said. She wasn't sure what made her choose her grandmother's name. It was the first thing that popped into her mind when he asked, and somehow it was oddly comforting.

"Vaida." He said her name as if it were a statement, reaching out to shake her hand. "I'm Cody."

"Nice to meet you," she said, her voice soft.

"You know, my uncle has a place across town. I could see about getting you on there. He always has openings. You interested?"

"That would be amazing," she said.

"It's not bartending. It would be waitressing or maybe

cooking. He owns a small diner. I can't promise anything, but he owes me a few favors."

She tried not to hop in place. "Thank you so much."

He nodded. "You look like you need the help. Do you want to just leave me your number? I can call you when I have an answer."

She glanced behind her as someone else entered the bar. It was a woman, no one she recognized, and yet she couldn't help feeling on edge. "Um," she said, not wanting to explain to him why an adult in 2019 wouldn't have a cellphone.

"I'm not hitting on you," he said blatantly with a laugh. "I'm totally gay. I just want to help."

"Oh, no, it's not that," she said. "I just...I don't have a phone. I'm—" She paused, not sure what to tell him, but she desperately needed a job and he seemed to be her only hope. Wasn't that just like her? On her own for only a day and already indebted to a man. "I'm kind of out on my own for the first time, and I'm not like a junkie or anything, I just don't have a lot of money. Any money, really. Which is why I need the job. So I can get a phone and a place to stay until I figure everything out." Should she have said that? "Not that I'll be leaving in a hurry." Great, now she was lying. "I just, I really need a job."

He nodded. "You don't have a place to stay either?"

She frowned. "I'm pretty pathetic, right? I'll figure something out though, I swear. As long as I can find some work, it'll all be okay." She winced. "I'm sorry. I know how this all sounds."

He turned around, filling a clear glass with tap water and sliding her a bowl of nuts. "Here, you look hungry. I get off in a few hours. You can crash with me for a bit until you get on your feet. That way I know where to find you if my uncle has an opening."

"What? Why would you help me?" she asked, staring at the water. She couldn't deny how dry her throat was or how her stomach was rumbling just staring at the bowl of peanuts. "You don't even know me. I could be crazy." Now, why the hell would she say that?

"Are you crazy?" he asked.

"No," she said plainly. "Well, no more than the average person."

He smirked. "For all you know, I'm crazy, too." That was true, she hadn't even stopped to worry about the very thing that had put her in this position in the first place. Cody could want to hurt her. Just like he *had. "But if you'll trust me, I'll trust you."*

"I don't know," she said. "It's a sweet offer, but I couldn't put you out like that."

"It's no trouble, Vaida. My roommate just moved out, and I'm looking for a new one. If you get this job, we can split rent. If not, you can crash for a few days while you get everything worked out. It's not a big deal."

"Are you serious?" she asked, raising her eyebrows and grabbing a peanut.

"As a heart attack, baby," he said, patting the counter. "One rule though." He held up a finger.

"What's that?"

"I need a Netflix binge-watching partner. Hating trashy TV would be my only deal breaker." He smiled. "You in?"

She smiled, reaching out and shaking his hand once again. "I'm in."

EIGHTEEN

GAVIN

"What do you mean they're looking for you?" Gavin repeated, staring into Vaida's haunted eyes.

She shook her head. "We have to go."

"They could be out there, watching to see if we're going to come out. We can't leave. Not yet."

"You're trying to protect me?" she asked.

"Of course I am. Why wouldn't I?"

"I've just told you the cops are looking for me, Gavin."

"Don't you mean Fletcher? Oh, no wait, I am Gavin," he said, feigning confusion. "Have you not heard anything I've told you? The police are looking for me, too. I'm not exactly citizen of the year, Vaida. Whatever you've done, I can help you."

She closed her eyes, looking away from him. "You can't. You can't be involved in this. I can't put you in danger—"

"I can take care of myself," he said defiantly. "More than

that, I can take care of you." His voice softened. "If you'll let me."

She looked back at him, her eyes filled with tears. "I don't need anyone to take care of me."

"I know that," he said. "That's what I find so...*enticing* about you. I know you don't need me. And yet, here you are."

She squinted at him. "You find me enticing?"

He nodded. "Would I be here with you if I didn't?"

"I thought you were here with me because you needed a car." She looked at him skeptically.

He smirked. "Or maybe I needed a car because I wanted to be here with you."

"Gavin, I—"

"Shh," he quieted her, his eyes locked on hers. "Whatever you've done, whatever you are running from...I can help you. But, you have to trust me."

She shook her head slowly. "I don't trust anyone."

"And yet, here you are. On this road trip with someone you hardly know." He leaned in, reaching a hand for her cheek. "Could it be because you find me *enticing* as well?"

She shook her head again, though she didn't break eye contact. "I can't—"

"You can," he said. "If you want. You can tell me the truth. All of it. Because I care about you, Vaida. And right now I feel like I would go to the ends of the earth to protect you if that's what it takes. Because I see in your eyes something I've seen in my own for years now."

"What's that?" she asked, her eyes moving to his lips.

"Fear," he whispered. "And incredible loneliness." She nodded, her lips parting. "Maybe our 'brokens' need each other."

"Gavin," she whispered.

He moved his hand further onto her cheek, his fingers tangled in her hair as he leaned in. "I like the way you say my name." His breathing was growing erratic as their lips grew closer together. Neither of them fought what they both knew was coming. "You're one of the only people in my life who knows the real one."

"I'm dangerous," she said, her lips brushing his.

"I've never been afraid of a little danger." He pulled her face to his, their lips crashing together with long-awaited passion. In the tiny car, there was hardly room for them to move, their breath hot against each other's skin, but he pulled her across the seat and onto his lap without a second thought. She let out a sigh, hitting her head on the ceiling and cursing.

"What are we doing?" she asked, though her mouth was on his again before he could answer.

He cupped her neck with one hand, his kisses growing more ravenous, as his other hand slid down beside the seat, searching for the lever that would give them more room. He pressed the button, the seat jerking back instantly from their weight. She laughed, her teeth on his bottom lip.

He looked at her, the goddess in front of him, and his chest grew tight. *Among other things.* "God, you're beautiful," he told her, moving a piece of hair back from her eyes.

She let out a breath, her gaze dancing over him as a small smile filled her face. She traced a finger across his lips. "You aren't so bad yourself."

He held eye contact as he leaned in, pressing his lips to her jaw bone. She let out a moan that had him rock hard against his pants. His kisses traveled down her neck slowly, listening to her moans as she moved against him. He pulled the straps of her dress off her shoulders with cautious hands, kissing her warm skin, his tongue tracing her collar bone.

Her breaths were growing quicker in his ear, her chest rising and falling against his mouth. The windows in the car were completely fogged over and they could be caught at any moment, but Gavin couldn't have cared less. If this was it—this was how he went down, he was very much okay with that.

He pulled her dress down, his hands on her breasts instantly. She ran her hands through her hair, throwing her head back as he moved his mouth over them. She looked down, fire in her eyes, and began unbuttoning his shirt. He kissed her again, his head pounding as their kisses grew even more intense.

Gavin hadn't had sex in a car since he was a teenager, and the tiny space was no more comfortable than he remembered, but nothing could stop him from taking Vaida for his own. He pulled his shirt off as she undid the last button, her mouth immediately on his skin. Her lips were like butter as they made their way across his chest.

She pulled away, running a finger along the scars with a question in her eyes. He closed his eyes, swallowing hard. Without waiting for an answer, she leaned in, kissing each of them slowly. Gavin had never felt so exposed, yet completely turned on, in his life. She ran her nails down his chest, harder than he expected, and he moaned, feeling himself grow harder. He pulled her dress over her head, wanting to see all of her.

She smiled down at him as his eyes traveled over her body, his jaw hanging open. He grasped her waist, helping her move as she grinded against him. He lifted up, searching for her mouth again. She obliged, kissing him quickly as her hands began unbuttoning his pants.

She pulled his boxers down, allowing his girth to spring free, and took him in her hands. Her hands were cool against his warmth, and he leaned back, closing his eyes as she began to stroke him slowly.

"Oh, god," he moaned, clenching his fists by his sides.

She left his lap, climbing over into the passenger's seat once again, never letting her hand stop moving. She pressed her lips onto him, swiping his most sensitive skin with her tongue in a way that had him rolling his eyes back into his head. He opened his eyes, looking down at her. She was propped up on her knees, giving him a perfect side view. His gaze traveled down her long body before making his way back up. Her dark eyes were locked on his as she took him in her mouth, and he gasped for air. He slid back in the seat, his whole body shaking. She pulled away, smiling brightly.

"Do you have a...?" She trailed off, running her finger down the inside of his leg.

"Mhm," he moaned, hardly able to speak as he reached in his back pocket and pulled out his wallet. He pulled the blue wrapper from where it had sat for over a year and laid it on the dashboard, reaching for the white, lace panties that were his only barrier.

She raised her eyebrows, sitting back in her seat and sliding her fingers underneath the fabric, pulling them off her hips and down her long, dark legs slowly. Her eyes never left his. It was the most sensual moment he'd ever experienced, watching her undress for him.

As she pulled the panties over her heels, he grabbed her

waist again, pulling her back on top of him. He grabbed the condom, tearing open the wrapper and pulling it over him. He was throbbing hard as he lifted her up, sliding her down on top of him. She let out a sound that was mixture of a laugh and a moan as her head went back again. She sat still for a moment, his length completely inside of her, before she looked back up at him. She pressed her mouth to his, their breathing in sync as she put one hand on the ceiling and began moving slowly. The noises escaping their throats were almost animal-like, and Gavin realized in that moment how much they'd both needed each other. How much they'd both needed this.

He took hold of her hips, lifting her up and pulsing into her warmth quickly. Her throaty cries turned into all out screams as she began to shake, losing herself into their passion. He pounded against her skin with his, their bodies and broken souls finding solace in each other as they came all at once before collapsing in a heap of heavy breaths and silent tears.

In that moment, chest rising and falling with heavy breaths, Gavin knew nothing about their relationship would ever be the same.

NINETEEN

GAVIN

It was still dark out when they arrived back in Atlanta, and Vaida was sleeping soundly in the passenger's seat. Gavin slowed down as he approached the part of town she'd finally revealed to him as her home, searching for the apartment name. When he saw it, he pulled up next to the curb.

He turned down the radio, touching her shoulder. "Hey," he said softly, not entirely sure he wanted to wake her. Waking her up would mean their time together was over. He was half-tempted to remain there all night, just to be with her a bit longer, but that seemed a bit stalkerish.

She stirred, turning her head and rubbing the back of her hand over her eyes. "What?" She yawned, looking around.

"We're home," he told her, pulling his hand from her shoulder.

She looked out the window, still seeming confused.

"Oh," she said, sitting up further. "Oh. You shouldn't have let me sleep the whole way. I told you I could drive some."

"I know," he said simply. "But you were snoring, so I figured you needed the rest more than I did."

She frowned, letting out a laugh. "I would argue that I don't snore, but I totally do, so...yeah. Thank you for letting me sleep."

"My pleasure."

"Don't you want to go to your apartment first? I could drop you off."

"I can walk from here," he said. "It's not too far. I didn't want you to have to drive anymore than you need to."

"You don't need to walk through downtown Atlanta at," she paused, glancing at the dashboard clock, "three in the morning. Let me drive you home."

"I can take care of myself, Vaida. You don't have to worry about me."

She brushed the hair out of her face. "Okay."

"Thank you again for going with me." He leaned in, kissing her on the lips.

"Anytime, G-*Fletcher*," she said. "I guess I'd better get used to calling you that again, huh?"

He smiled sadly. "'Fraid so."

"Hey, Gavin?" she asked after a moment.

"Yeah?"

"Can I ask you something?"

He nodded, studying her face. "Anything."

"Back at your brother's house, he mentioned you have an ID with the name Fletcher on it, right?"

"Yeah," he confirmed. She paused, looking away and rubbing her neck. "What is it, Vaida?"

"I just...I wondered...how? How did you get one?" She looked back at him, and the icy fear was back.

"Do you need a fake ID?" he asked, cocking his head to the side. Parts of her story were starting to come together for him.

She ran a finger over her lips. "I think I might."

He nodded. "Okay. Well, to answer your question, I got mine from a friend who lives in New York now. He's a crime scene cleaner. Cleans up after dead bodies and stuff. Super gross. Anyway, he has guys on the inside that will sell him the IDs from some of the bodies he cleans up after. It's how I got me and Gia our new lives. His younger brother was in my class, and I knew him from around town. He used to sell fake IDs in highschool, way less quality than these, but enough to buy us alcohol or whatever. After Gia and I had been gone awhile, we tracked him down in hopes of finding a new ID."

"Do you think he could get me one? I mean, I don't have a lot of money right now, but I could save up."

"I'm sure he could. Ryan's a good guy. He even got my brother a job working with him as a favor to me after Gunner moved to New York." He paused, not meaning to have revealed that. "Shit. Gunner doesn't know that, so please don't tell him. He never wanted my help, and he also thought I was dead at the time," he said with a smile, "but he was really struggling when he moved there, and I always felt responsible, so I called in a favor. But, that stays between us."

She ran her fingers over her lips as if she were zipping a zipper. "Between the two of our crazy lives, we would make one hell of a reality show."

He kissed her. "Yeah, you can say that again. So, about

our crazy lives, are you going to tell me why you need a fake ID? Or am I just supposed to get you one on blind faith?"

She pressed her lips together. "I just...I'm not ready yet."

"Not ready for what?"

"For you to look at me like the monster I am," she said plainly.

He stared at her, his eyes stinging at her words. "Vaida, I could never look at you as anything other than the beautiful, smart, funny woman sitting right in front of me."

"You don't know what I've—"

"I don't care what you've done. I don't care who you were a second before you walked into that diner." He took a breath. "Because the second I laid eyes on you...I knew you were special. I knew you were going to be important in my life. I had no idea how hard and fast I would fall for you, but—"

"Fall for me?" she asked, her eyes wide.

"Yes. I know it's too soon, I know it doesn't make sense, but I am. I am falling for you."

"Stop," she said firmly, leaning away from him. "Please, please just stop."

"I'm sorry. I don't want to scare you off. It's been so long since I've felt this way about anyone, I'm not in any hurry. You don't have to feel the same way, I just want to be honest with you about how I'm feeling. I'll always want to be honest with you. I—"

"No," she said, holding her hand up. "Please don't. You can't feel that way about me, Gavin. I'm sorry. I've let you believe we could have a future, but the truth is we never can."

"What are you talking about? What about earlier? We

were amazing together. I thought you felt what I was feeling." At the moment, what he was feeling was a lump forming in his throat as he held back tears.

"Earlier was...a mistake." She closed her eyes as she delivered the blow. "We were in the heat of the moment, and I let myself get carried away. I should've stopped it. I didn't realize how you were feeling, but I should have. I'm sorry I misled you." He shook his head, unable to believe the words she was saying. No words could be formed as he stared at her unreadable face. "I'm sorry," she repeated. "I really am. You should go."

He nodded, rubbing his mouth, trying to keep his resolve. He pulled at the car door handle, turning on the overhead light, and climbed out of the car. She made no move to stop him as he shut the door, casting one last look at her before he headed down the street. After a few moments, he heard her car door opening and closing, its echo filling the quiet street. He slowed his steps, waiting for her to say his name, waiting to hear her beautiful voice, but it never happened. Instead, he walked alone, trying to hold his head up as his heart was ripped from his chest.

TWENTY

GAVIN

The next day, Gavin was awoken by the sound of his front door slamming shut. He sat up on the couch, the blanket falling down to his lap.

"Sorry, bro, didn't realize you were still asleep," Jaxon said. He stood in front of Gavin, his gym clothes soaked with sweat, earbuds still in his ears. He was breathing heavy, further evidence that he'd made his morning run already.

"You're up early," Gavin said groggily.

"It's ten a.m., dude," he said, taking a swig from his water bottle. "Rough night?"

Gavin rubbed his eyes, looking at the clock. "You could say that."

"I thought you were gonna be gone awhile," he said, sitting down on the couch and taking another drink.

"Plans changed," Gavin said. "I'll probably call Burt and see if I can get my old shifts back."

Jaxon shook his head. "So, you gonna spill the dirty details?"

"What are you talking about?"

"Vaida, man. I heard she went with you."

"Oh," Gavin said, her name stinging his chest. "Nothing to tell." He threw his legs over the edge of the couch, the concrete floor cold on his feet. A loud yawn escaped his throat as he stood and headed for the kitchen.

"Yeah, right," Jaxon said. Gavin grabbed the coffee from the cabinet, filling the pot and turning it on. He rubbed his eyes, sleep still clouding them, and pulled a coffee cup down from the shelf. He felt as though he were in a fog and Vaida was the last thing he wanted to discuss with Jaxon. But, as usual, his roommate was persistent. "I know that's not true. You are totally into her, man. Tell me you made a move on that."

Gavin shrugged. "It didn't matter. She isn't into me."

"Oh, shit, sorry," Jaxon said, standing up and walking to the island. "What happened?"

"It doesn't matter. I don't want to talk about it." Gavin shrugged, pouring his coffee before the pot was full.

"Right," Jaxon said, slapping the counter. "Well, her loss. I guess that means I get my wingman back, right? Let's get you back on the *whores*." He gave him a sly smile. "I'm hitting this club tonight if you want to hang."

Gavin shook his head, but stopped himself short. "Actually, yeah. You know what? I will go."

"Way to go, Fletch," Jaxon said, nodding his head with pride, his top teeth biting his bottom lip. "All right, I'm gonna jump in the shower before work. You need in there?"

"No, go ahead," Gavin said, taking a drink of his too-hot

coffee. He leaned up against the counter, letting the caffeine warm him. He wasn't usually a black coffee drinker, but his usual two creams and one sugar over ice just didn't sound good this morning. Nothing sounded good. Nothing except her. Gavin allowed himself to realize that Vaida had filled the giant hole in his life, the one that Holly had left not so long ago. He never thought he could find anyone who would make him feel the way she had, but something in Vaida connected with him—perhaps that they were both broken beyond repair. Did broken souls seek each other out? Was he destined to always love a woman who would destroy him?

As the shower kicked on, a knock sounded on the front door. Gavin set his mug down on the concrete countertop and walked toward the door. He swung it open, still half asleep, and stared into the face of a police officer with red hair and bloodshot blue eyes.

Gavin's breath caught, and he felt the blood drain from his face. He cleared his throat, trying to keep calm. "Um, can I help you?"

"Jaxon Roth?" the officer asked.

"Um, no, he's in the shower. Do you need him?" He used his thumb to point over his shoulder.

The cop shook his head. "Who are you?"

"Fletcher, his roommate."

"Well, Fletcher, his roommate," he said with a snarky attitude, "do you have a last name?"

"Denali," he answered, his heart pounding so loudly he was sure the officer could hear it. Would he notice the sweat beading around his hairline? "Is something wrong?"

"Can I come in?" the officer asked.

Gavin hesitated. "I'd like to know what this is about,

please," he told him, not moving as the man tried to enter the apartment.

"Either you or your roommate were seen with a young woman early this morning near First Street."

"Is there a question in there?" He was growing increasingly annoyed with the officer's vagueness.

"Was it you or your roommate?" he asked, the words filled with agitation.

"I'm not sure. I mean, I guess it was me."

"You guess?"

"Look, can you just tell me what's going on?"

The officer sighed, scratching his forehead. "Was the girl a friend of yours?"

"I'm not telling you anything else until you answer my question. What is going on?" He wasn't sure if his words were going to get him into trouble, but he wasn't going to divulge anything else without a reason.

The officer's face was grim. "I'm sorry to tell you this, son, but your friend was found murdered this morning."

TWENTY-ONE

GAVIN

Gavin allowed the officer into the apartment, his head in a fog. He listened as the man explained the circumstances of Vaida's death: a hit and run. Drunk driver most likely. He touched Gavin's shoulder when he said the words in what must have been an attempt to seem sympathetic, but it just made Gavin more angry.

His stomach was a pit of venom. Everything in him bubbled with anger, and yet he could not move, could not speak. He felt the officer's eyes still on him, trying to read his reaction, but he could no longer meet the man's gaze. Why had he left Vaida alone last night? Why had he let her run him off? He could've protected her. It was his fault she was out that late anyway. It was all his fault. Again, the death of a woman he loved was entirely his fault.

He clenched his jaw, looking at the officer finally. "Is

there," he cleared his throat, "is there anything else I can do for you?"

"I just have a few questions."

He nodded, looking away. "Go ahead."

"What was the young woman's name?"

"Don't you know that?"

"Her ID was missing from her body when we arrived at the scene," he said. "We're waiting on the results from her fingerprint panel to come back if she's in the system, but we wanted to see if you could fill us in sooner. So we can alert her family."

"Her name was Vaida," he said finally. "But I don't believe she has—*had* any family."

The man scribbled down notes. "Last name?"

"I, um," he paused, suddenly feeling protective of Vaida and the secrets she couldn't share with him. "I don't know."

"You don't know?"

"I don't remember."

The man stared at him for a moment. "And how did you know this Vaida?"

"We worked together," Gavin told him. "At Burt's. It's a diner across town."

He wrote the name of the diner down. "Had you known her very long? Did she have any enemies that you knew of?"

"No, we hadn't known each other long. I don't know much about her life outside of work. I thought you said it was a drunk driver?"

"We're exploring all our options," he said simply.

"Am I an option?" he asked, raising an eyebrow.

The man shook his head. "The witness who called nine-one-one saw you walk away minutes before the car hit her."

"How would they have known where I lived then?"

"I don't know," he answered, seeming agitated. "Let's get back to the line of questioning. Do you know her address?"

"I don't," Gavin said. "I know her apartment building, it's called Park Street Apartments, but I have no idea what number. Are you checking into the witness? That seems suspicious to me."

"Leave the detective work to the professionals, son. I promise you we're going to do everything we can to make sure justice is served." He paused. "Okay," he said, "one last question, do you have any idea what made the victim relocate to Atlanta? Was she running from something?"

"No," Gavin answered, though his blood suddenly ran cold. "No, I'm sorry, I don't know."

"Thank you," the officer said, folding up the notebook and slipping it into his pocket. He pulled out a blank card and wrote his number onto it. "If you think of anything, you'll give me a call, right?"

"Yes, I will." He eyed the card. "Blank cards?"

"Budget cuts," the officer explained, nodding as he headed for the door. Gavin watched him walk out, panic filling him. Everything about the officer's questioning had seemed strange. The police knew more than they were letting on. As he stood there, trying to decide his next move, one question kept floating through his mind. *If they hadn't known Vaida's name, how had they known she'd relocated to Atlanta?*

TWENTY-TWO

GAVIN

Gavin paced the halls of Vaida's apartment building, knocking on the doors to each apartment. Most inhabitants didn't answer, and the few who did were of very little help to him. He walked back down the stairs, stopping at the mailboxes to search for her name. Several pieces of mail were pinned to a bulletin board, but as he searched through them, he didn't find anything addressed to her. He sighed, shoving his hands down onto the counter. Realizing he was running out of options, he groaned. What on earth was he going to do? He couldn't give up on her, couldn't stop searching until he found his answers.

"Lose your mailbox key?" A stranger's voice carried through the quiet hall softly.

Gavin spun around. "Huh? Oh, no." He shook his head. "Sorry. I'm trying to find my friend's apartment."

"Oh," the man said, pulling his keys from his pocket and

walking to open his own mailbox. "What's the name? I might know 'em." He pulled out a stack of mail, flipping through it quickly before looking back up at Gavin.

"Um, Vaida," he said. "But, she...passed away. She used to live here."

"Why are you looking for her apartment, then? If she's not here anymore."

"It's stupid, I know," Gavin said. "I was hoping to find her roommate. She mentioned she had one. I wanted to talk to them."

The man stared at him a moment too long. "Wait a second," he said, "what did you say your name was?"

"I didn't," Gavin answered. When the stranger didn't respond, he grunted his name, not wanting to go through small talk when all he could think about was Vaida. "Fletcher."

"I'm Cody," he said, holding out a hand and shaking Gavin's firmly. "Come with me."

"Come with you?" Gavin asked. "Why?"

"Because I think I know which apartment your friend lived in." He was already halfway up the staircase, not turning to look and see if Gavin was following him. "Come on."

Huffing, Gavin followed him up the stairs, taking them two at a time in an attempt to keep up. When they reached the third floor, the man stopped, turning his key in a lock and opening the apartment door. "Come in," he said, holding it open.

"I thought you were taking me to Vaida's apartment."

"I've got it written down in here somewhere," he said. "I'll find it for you. No use standing out in the hallway."

Gavin bowed his head, walking into the apartment without time to worry about the decision. He looked around the small, airy apartment. A bottle of white wine sat on the counter, a sofa in the middle of the room, and a wine glass on the marble coffee table.

"Thank you for helping me," Gavin said as the door shut behind him.

"Not a problem." Cody's menacing growl was too close. Gavin spun around, just as something hard slammed into his head. He stumbled back, blinking his eyes to clear his vision just as another THWACK pounded against his temple.

As he crashed to the ground, he saw the blurry outline of Cody standing above him, a black cast iron skillet in his folded hands. And then, darkness found him.

TWENTY-THREE

VAIDA
THE NIGHT BEFORE

Vaida sat in the car, watching Gavin walk away and wanting desperately to stop him. Her heart ached as she saw him cock his head back toward her. He was waiting for her to call out to him, and everything in her knew that she couldn't.

She'd been foolish. Foolish for letting him get to her, foolish for letting herself believe she could be happy, that she could have a future with anyone ever again. Angry and heartbroken, she pushed open the car door and climbed out. She stood, watching him round a corner before she let out a breath she hadn't meant to be holding. A stray tear fell down her cheek, and she brushed it away.

Her body was filled with an unbridled rage at her situation and her heart for putting her there once again. She couldn't trust anyone, that was the rule. The one rule she had to follow. It was the only thing that would keep her alive, and she'd almost broken it. And for what? A goofy smile and dark eyes you could get lost in? She rolled her own eyes, thinking about his. What was she doing?

Just like that, she was lost in her thoughts of his smile, thoughts about how it felt to have his arms around her, how his lips felt on hers. Her insides grew warm at the thought of him, and suddenly she knew she'd made a grave mistake. Why on earth had she let him go? The one man she might be able to trust? The one man whose secret was so eerily similar to her own.

She took off in a dead run, hurrying down the sidewalk in the direction of his apartment. She was being ridiculous, she knew. She could drive to his apartment, explain it all, but instead she found freedom in her run. It seemed like it had been years since she'd last been able to run for pleasure, though she'd once enjoyed it very much. She rounded the corner, looking both ways before she crossed the street. Gavin was already gone, but she would run to his apartment building if that's what it took. She would do whatever it took to make it right.

She turned at the next block, her lungs beginning to burn. As she crossed the pavement, a vehicle turned onto the street, its headlights illuminating the night around her. She paused, staring into the bright lights as the engine revved up. They were headed right toward her, despite being on the wrong side of the road. Something about the truck had her staring a moment too long. Did she recognize it? As it grew closer, she stepped up onto the sidewalk and out of the way.

The truck swerved as it neared her and the scream that escaped her throat was filled with pure, unequivocal fear.

TWENTY-FOUR

GAVIN

Gavin's head radiated pain, his eyelids heavy. He blinked, attempting to move his hand to his head, but it wouldn't budge. As his vision began to come into focus, the morning's events came back to him. Vaida was gone. Dead. And he had walked into a stranger's apartment in an attempt to find her. In front of him, a blurry dark figure sat. He crossed his arms, leaning back in his chair as his face grew clear.

Cody. "What the fuck, man?" Gavin asked, wincing. "What are you doing?"

Cody stood. "I should be asking you the same question," he said. "*What did you do?*"

"Excuse me?" he demanded. "What are you talking about?" His head throbbed with every word, parts of the room still dizzy and out of focus.

He took a step toward Gavin. "I said...*what did you do?*"

His face grew red as his voice filled with anger. "What did you do with her?"

"What? With who?" Gavin asked, recognizing the pain that was suddenly on his face. "With Vaida? Wait, did you know Vaida?" Hope filled him as he asked the questions.

"Don't play dumb with me, asshole. I know you and Vaida went out of town. I know you were the last person to see her alive. So, either tell me what you did with her, or I'm calling the police and you can tell them."

"What the hell are you talking about?" Gavin's confusion was growing as his head continued to pound. The man in front of him was a complete stranger, yet they seemed to have one thing in common—they had both cared about Vaida.

"That's it," Cody said, grabbing his phone from the counter. "I'm calling the police. That girl did not deserve whatever you've done to her. She trusted you, man. She liked you. How sick of a person do you have to be to prey on young women? Sickos like you are exactly why women are so afraid. But, not me. I'm not afraid of you, and I'm damn sure not letting you go until you tell me what you've done." He was shaking as he stared at Gavin, so many questions in his eyes.

"I didn't hurt Vaida," Gavin insisted. "You've got it all wrong. I cared about her. I cared about her so much." He hung his head with sorrow. "I never wanted any of this to happen."

"It was all an accident, right? I'm sure they've never heard that one before." He rolled his eyes, one hand on his hip.

Gavin looked back up. "I didn't do anything, man. I don't

know what the police have told you, but they think it was a drunk driver. I'm not even a suspect. I'm really sorry she's gone." He coughed as he felt his eyes begin to sting with fresh tears. "I am. Vaida was...she was special to me. I hadn't known her for very long, but I would've done anything to protect her. I swear to you I would've."

Cody frowned, crossing his arms. "You talked to the cops already?"

"Yes," Gavin told him. "They came to my apartment this morning."

"They told me they didn't know where to find you." He rubbed his hand over his jaw, looking away.

"They talked to you, too? *Who are you?*"

He set down his cellphone, taking a seat back in the chair. "I'm Cody," he told him. "Vaida's roommate."

"The one who got her a job a Burt's?" he asked, remembering the conversation.

"Burt is my uncle." He nodded, crossing one leg over the other. "I don't understand how they found you. And I don't understand why you aren't in custody."

"I told you, I haven't done anything wrong. They had a witness that saw me leave before it happened."

"Before *what* happened?"

"Before she was hit," he said softly, twisting his head to the side.

"Hit?" Cody looked baffled. "Hit by what?"

Gavin closed his eyes, trying to ward off the headache that was growing more painful by the second. "I'm confused," he said finally. "Don't you know what happened to her?"

"Of course not," he said. "That's why it's an investigation." He lowered his brow. "What do you know?"

He shook his head. "They told me she was hit by a car. That it was most likely a drunk driver."

"So, they found her?"

"Are we even talking about the same thing?"

"The police told me that Vaida was reported missing," Cody said. "I gave them your name and told them you'd left town together."

"That's it?"

"That's it."

Gavin shook his head. "What time did the police come to see you?"

"I don't know," he said, glancing at his phone screen. "Maybe around eight or nine?"

"An officer came to my apartment around ten and said that Vaida was killed in a hit and run," Gavin explained over Cody's gasp. "He told me they didn't even know her name, said her wallet was missing when they found her body."

"That's not possible," Cody said in a hushed voice. "He knew who she was. Why, the officer who came here even cleaned out some of her stuff from her room to help with the investigation."

"And they didn't mention anything about an accident to you?"

"Nothing at all. He said there was no reason to assume Vaida wasn't fine, and he gave me his card in case she showed up or I thought of anything that could help."

Gavin twisted his arms under the ropes that were bound around him. "Was it a blank card? One he wrote his number on?" Cody nodded. "I have the same one. It's in my pocket. If you'll untie me, I'll prove I'm telling the truth."

"Fat chance," Cody said loudly. "But if you are, then the police are lying to us."

"Now the only question is why?" Gavin asked.

"And what happened to Vaida?"

"Do me a favor," Gavin said, still squirming. The ropes had begun to rub a raw patch on his skin.

"I'm not letting you out yet."

"I don't care. I'm not going anywhere, regardless. Not until we figure this out. I need you to call the police."

"What are you talking about?"

"Call the Atlanta Police Department and ask to speak to someone on Vaida's case. Tell them you just wanted to see if there's been any updates."

"Why would I do that?"

"Just do it," Gavin growled. "Amuse me."

Cody placed his thumb on the iPhone's unlock button, searching for the police department's number and clicking on it to place the call. He pressed the speakerphone button. "If this is a trap—"

"Shhh," Gavin warned him as the automated system kicked on, warning them to call nine-one-one if they were experiencing an emergency. Cody made it through the prompts, clicking through to speak with an officer in Missing Persons.

"Atlanta Police Department, Missing Persons. What officer can I connect you with?" a stern voice came over the speaker.

"Uh, hi, yes. Um, I need to speak with an officer on a missing person's case."

"You're going to have to be more specific," came the snappy response.

"My friend, Vaida Williams, went missing this morning. An officer came to my apartment, but I've lost his number and I can't remember his name."

"Tell them you want an update," Gavin whispered.

"I just wanted to see if I could get an update. I'm really worried about her."

"I can assure you, our officers are doing all they can. Let me see what I can find out for you. Please hold."

"Okay, thank—"

The line was placed on hold before he could finish, and the two of them sat in silence, staring at each other while waiting for answers. After a moment, the voice came back. "Sir?"

"Yes?"

"We don't have any open missing persons cases for a Vaida Williams."

"Maybe it's a murder case? Her friend said the officer told him—"

"Sir, there are no open cases period for any Vaida Williams. Maybe it was another department. Now, if you'd like to come in and file a report, you can, but I'm afraid I'm not able to help you out any more than that."

"Oh," Cody said, staring at the phone in horror. "Maybe you know the officer? Red hair, super pale? Blue eyes?"

"That's not ringing any bells," the man said. "I'm sorry. You can stop by and see if we can help you track him down if you'd like." He paused. "I've got to go. Hopefully you find the card."

With that, the line went dead and Cody looked up at

Gavin. "Why are you smiling?" he asked, covering his mouth. "This is horrible."

"Because that's exactly what I was hoping would happen."

"What are you talking about?"

"Whoever came to talk to us today wasn't a cop. At least not an Atlanta one. And they've just told you there is no open case for Vaida. Which explains why we were given separate stories about what happened."

"Explains it how?" Cody asked.

"The man we met, cop or not, was trying to get as much information about Vaida from us as possible. But he wasn't counting on us ever meeting to make sure his story lined up."

"I'm sorry, I'm lost. His story?"

"About what happened to Vaida."

"What *did* happen to Vaida?"

"I don't know," Gavin said. "But whatever it was, I don't believe we were given the truth. Which means it's up to us to find out what the truth is."

"Up to us?" Cody placed his fingertips on his chest in shock. "No, honey. I don't even know you. There is no *us*. Besides that, I didn't really even know Vaida."

"You knew her enough to knock me over the head to protect her."

"Yeah, well, my gramma always said there ain't no use keeping a cast iron skillet around if you can't use it to knock some sense into people now and again." He smirked.

"If you don't want to help me, I can't make you. But you do have to let me go. Unless your plan is to kill me."

"I do want to help you. I just can't decide if I can trust you," he said thoughtfully.

"If I was lying...I wouldn't have been right about the police not having Vaida's case. We need to find out who the man was who approached us and why he was impersonating a cop. Then, we need to find out what happened to Vaida."

"Okay, I'll untie you," Cody said finally, standing up. "But, I'm holding onto this." He picked up the black skillet from the floor and held it up. "You try anything and I'll hit you again. And this time, I *will* call the police on you."

Gavin nodded. "I'm not a threat to you."

Cody approached him slowly, one hand on the skillet the whole time as he attempted to untie him. "Hold still," Cody said, struggling with the ropes.

"Why did you have ropes lying around anyway?" Gavin asked.

"Wouldn't you like to know," Cody said with a wink as the ropes fell free.

Gavin scooted forward in his chair, shaking his hands and rubbing the feeling back into his wrists. There were red and purple ligature marks ensnaring his arms. He leaned over, helping Cody untie his ankles before standing up.

Cody stood in front of him, their eyes locking together. "So, what do we do now?" he asked.

"You're going to help me?"

"Vaida wasn't the warmest roommate I've ever had, but that doesn't mean I wanted anything bad to happen to her."

Gavin nodded. "Okay, well, first thing's first...we need to figure out who the man was that approached us both. We can try to reverse phone search the number he gave us."

Cody nodded, walking toward the kitchen. Gavin followed close behind, his gaze searching around the rooms where Vaida had lived. It made him miss her more.

An identical business card to the one Gavin had been given was hanging on the stainless steel refrigerator. Cody pulled it from the magnet, grabbing his phone from his pocket and typing it in. He scrolled for a moment, his thumb running over the screen. Finally, he shook his head, handing the phone over. "I don't know what I'm looking for. It shows the carrier here and a few names but they're all different."

Gavin looked over the screen. He was right, there were several. "We'll have to check into all of them, then."

"Do you have any idea how long that will take?"

"Do you have a deadline for helping Vaida?" Gavin asked testily.

"No, but, I'm just saying...I mean, look. I want to help her, I do. I want justice and I want answers. But, if she's gone, what does any of it matter? She's dead, Fletcher. We can't change that."

"Unless she isn't," he said, spitting out the one last hope he had left. "And even if she is, we can't just let it be over like that."

"What are you talking about?"

"I need to know the truth," he said. "I need to know what happened to her, and I need to know why that man lied to us."

"Who is this really for?" Cody asked, cocking his head to the side. "Is it for Vaida? Or is it for you?"

Gavin shook his head, handing back the phone. "You don't have to help me."

"You're avoiding the quest—"

"I don't know," Gavin insisted. "I don't know who this is for, and I don't know what I'm hoping to find out, but I do know that I can't just accept what has happened without digging. I can't." He let out a sigh.

"You really did care about her, didn't you?"

He pressed his lips together, not wanting to seem vulnerable but unable to deny his feelings. "Yeah. I really *do*."

TWENTY-FIVE

GAVIN

Gavin searched through the list of every person who had ever owned the number the officer had given them. He narrowed it down, sorting through ones who he could look up using Cody's Facebook app. None of the people were the officer.

He sighed, taking another drink of the beer Cody had offered him a half hour ago. They were running out of options. And time. Hell, they were running out of hope. "I don't know what else to look for," he said eventually, scratching his head.

"I mean, it's possible this number is just unlisted, right? Maybe cops don't put their numbers out there like regular people."

Gavin shrugged. "Maybe."

"Maybe. Or maybe he gave us a fake number."

"That doesn't make any sense."

"We could try to call it," Cody said, standing up and walking to the window. He looked out at the street.

"I don't want to tip him off if we don't have to."

"I'll just ask for an update."

Gavin stood, too, needing to stretch his legs. "I just don't understand how she could simply disappear without anyone knowing anything."

"Hang on a second," Cody said suddenly, turning around and grabbing his phone. "There may be something in her room that could help." He walked to Vaida's bedroom and twisted the knob, pushing open the door swiftly.

"What are we doing?"

"Just come here," he said, approaching a small white desk on the far side of the room. The bedroom was small, a twin sized bed in the middle of the room with a simple white comforter on it. There was nothing left in the room that would've claimed Vaida, nothing left to prove she ever existed.

Cody was digging through the drawers, the air around them eerily still. "What are you looking for?" Gavin asked.

"Ah-hah!" Cody said, pulling out a thick piece of cardstock from between two books. It had an address written in hurried pencil, the handwriting familiar. "This."

"What is it?" Gavin asked. He recognized the curly Es and the capital Rs that Vaida used at work when writing orders.

"An address."

"I can see that. Whose address?" He moved closer, taking a breath as he saw the address was in Dakota. "Hers?"

"I don't know," Cody said, turning it over in his hand. "To be honest, I didn't know much about her at all. She wasn't exactly...open about herself. But, she did write a letter once. To this address. I came home early, and her bedroom door was open. She shoved this in her drawer and ran down to the mailbox with an envelope in her hand." He looked down. "I'm not normally one to snoop, but not knowing anything about her...well, it drove me crazy."

"You went through her things?"

"Don't judge," Cody snapped. "It's a good thing I did. This might be the only clue we have to helping us find out the truth about what happened to her. Maybe whoever she sent that letter to...maybe they can help us."

Gavin took the paper. "So, we go there?"

"I was thinking something a bit simpler."

"Like?"

"Like Google," he said. "No need for a road trip when we have a little thing called the internet." He typed the address into his phone, holding it out to Gavin with a smile. "Looks like this address belongs to a Joy Westerfield. Ever heard of her?"

"No, have you?" He handed the phone back.

"No," Cody said. "But, my guess is she can tell us more about Vaida than we could ever find through our own pitiful investigation." He looked down at the screen again.

"So, let's look her up."

Cody nodded. "Already done. There's only one Joy Westerfield in Dakota, Georgia." He smirked. "Lucky her name wasn't Ann Smith. Should I send her a message?"

"Yeah," Gavin said reluctantly. "Ask her if she is the woman Vaida wrote to?"

He nodded, texting the message. "Look, she's typing

already." He smiled. "This might actually work." His smile faded. "No, the message stopped."

"What?" Gavin asked.

"It went away. She's not saying anything now."

"How do you know?"

"The bubbles are..." He trailed off, noticing Gavin's lost expression. "You don't have Facebook, do you? She was right."

"Who was right?"

"Vaida. When we looked you up, she said you probably didn't—"

"You looked me up?" He raised a brow, and suddenly Cody looked shy.

"Yeah, sorry. She, um, well...I was curious who had my girl smiling like she was." He grinned. Gavin's face warmed up, and instantly he felt tears in his eyes. He looked down, coughing to avoid the silence. "She really liked you, Fletcher. She didn't want to admit it, and she never opened up to me...but I could tell."

Gavin looked back up, grabbing the paper from him. "We aren't waiting around."

"What? What are you talking about?" Cody asked, following him as he left Vaida's room.

"I'm going to Dakota, and I'm going to make this Joy woman talk to us. I'm going to make her tell me everything she knows about Vaida."

"What are you going to do? Just show up at her house?"

"That's exactly what I'm going to do," Gavin said, swinging open the door. "Now, are you coming with me or not?"

Cody sighed. "I need to pack a bag."

"You have five minutes," Gavin said, checking the time on his phone.

"Don't you need to pack anything?"

"Right now my priority is finding a car. Is Vaida's still out there?"

Cody shook his head. "The cops took it this morning."

"Well then, we'll need to take yours."

Cody turned his head, staring at him. "Oh, that's right."

"What's right?"

He pursed his lips, a smile growing on his face. "You're the scrub."

TWENTY-SIX

GAVIN

The boys arrived in Dakota, Georgia, the next morning. It had been a long, taxing drive sitting next to a stranger, and Gavin was ready to get out of the car. During the time that Cody slept, snoring loudly from the passenger's side, Gavin had allowed himself to process what was happening. Why the hell was he headed to Dakota, anyway? It made no difference if he found out what happened to Vaida. Except somewhere in his heart was hope, the slightest little hope, that somehow he could save her. That somehow the cop was wrong. That his lie was just that...a complete lie. After all, he'd lied about who he was, why not about what had happened?

He couldn't keep her face out of his head, her small smile; the way her dark eyes could look so deep into his, it was like she could see all his innermost thoughts. Small tears kept forming in his eyes, reminding him that he'd lost someone else. Someone else he cared about. Someone else he might've loved. How was he ever going to survive this?

Holly's death had destroyed him. It ripped every human part out of him, leaving an empty, callous shell. Most days, he struggled with the idea that he would've been better off gone, and it was only pure fear that kept him from ending his life. Holly had been it for him, his entire world, and Gia had stolen that—and any chance at being happy—away from him.

But, that all changed the moment he saw Vaida. It was instant. It wasn't as if he'd never seen another beautiful girl. The city was full of them. It was...something about Vaida. Her eyes, her presence...it was the same thing he'd seen in Holly. Something that connected with his soul. Something that could make him think thoughts like this. Something that could make him drive nearly two hours away just for the slight possibility of finding her. Of saving her.

It was a long shot. Practically impossible. No, scratch that, *literally* impossible. Vaida was...he couldn't bring himself to even think the word. He wasn't sure he'd survive this again. Losing someone...losing everyone was just too hard. What was the point anymore? Everyone in his life was gone. Everyone.

He wiped away a stray tear as he pulled onto the street where they should be able to find Joy Westerfield. He parked in front of a small brick home with navy blue shutters and nudged Cody. "Wake up."

Cody moved slowly, stretching his arms above his head and yawning loudly. He glanced around, blinking his heavy eyelids. "We made it?" he asked.

"We made it," Gavin confirmed, pointing to the house. The small, paved driveway was inviting, and the flowerbeds gave him hope that the woman inside may be able to help them, but he couldn't deny the dread that filled his stomach. "You coming with me?"

Cody nodded. "Might as well." And then, as Gavin opened the door, he heard Cody's voice again. "Do you have a plan?"

He slammed the door shut, already walking toward the house. "Nope, not at all."

Behind him, he heard Cody's door shut and then his hurried footsteps approaching him. "You're just going to knock on her door? Without a plan?"

He nodded, reaching out to knock on the dark blue door. "Yep, something like that."

The house was silent. Gavin listened carefully for footsteps. Out of the corner of his eye, he saw the curtains move in the window to his right. He jerked his head in that direction, stepping into the flower garden so he could peer through the glass of the window. The curtains snapped shut before he could see the inhabitant. He darted back to the door, knocking louder. "I know you're in there," he called.

"Well, that's certainly not going to make her answer the door," Cody said snarkily from behind him.

"Joy? Is it Joy?" he called, ignoring Cody.

"Great, now we seem like stalkers, too. Perfect."

"Will you shut up?" Gavin asked, placing his ear to the door. "I'm here about my friend. Vaida Williams. Did you know her?"

Movement. He heard movement just beyond the door. "Please. Please just open up and talk to us."

Finally, the door swung open and a woman with short,

graying blonde hair stuck her head in the crack. "What do you want? I have nine-one-one on speed dial."

Gavin held up his hands. "We mean you no harm." He waited for her to open the door further, but she didn't. "Are you Joy Westerfield?"

"Depends on who's asking."

"My name's Fletcher. This is Cody. We think you may know our friend...Vaida?"

She lowered her brow, making a move to shut the door. "Nope. Don't know any Vaidas."

Gavin held out his hand, stopping the door from shutting completely. "Are you sure? Because we think she wrote you a letter."

"I don't know anything about anything," she said hastily, pushing the door harder against Gavin's hand. He didn't budge.

"So, you don't know that she's dead?"

The woman wavered, her eyes growing wide as she sucked in a breath. Within seconds, she had regained her composure and shook her head. "What did you say?"

"Vaida. The woman you *don't* know...she's dead." He shook his head, shrugging. "I thought you'd want to know."

She opened the door wider. "I don't understand."

"Vaida was—"

"How did you know Vaida?"

"She was my friend," he said softly, noticing the tears that were now lining her blue eyes. "In Atlanta."

"Atlanta?" she asked, her voice cracking. "She...I'm sorry." She lowered her head, looking away. "I'm sorry. I have to go."

"Please," Gavin said, though he finally let go of the door.

"Please, if you knew her...we're just trying to find out the truth about what happened to her. If you knew her...if you cared about her...I would think you would want that, too."

She didn't move to shut the door, staring in between Gavin and Cody before she finally sighed. "You should come inside."

GAVIN SAT NEXT to Cody on the brown leather sofa in Joy's living room. She sat in front of them, her jaw tight, hands wound together.

"If you can give us any information about Vaida, about her life here before she moved to Atlanta, it could really help us."

"How did she...how did she die?" Joy asked, unable to look them in the eye.

"We—" Gavin paused, clearing his throat. "We don't really know."

"What do you mean?"

"The police think it was a hit and run," Gavin told her, choosing to keep the story simple. "But, we aren't so sure." He stared at her, trying to read her expression. "Look, I know you don't owe us anything, but Cody was Vaida's roommate. He says he saw her writing you letters, or *a* letter at least. That must mean she meant something to you, right? If you could just...just tell us more about her, it would help. It could help us figure out what happened. It could help us get justice for Vaida."

She nodded, running a finger over her lip and taking a deep breath before she began. "I didn't know her well anymore," she said finally. "But I did care about her. I'm sad to hear she's gone. But, I'm afraid I don't have much to tell you about her."

"How did you know her?"

"She was—" She paused, looking to the window. "She was my neighbor. For several years. At one point, we were close, but that changed a few years ago. Lately, we only saw each other in passing, waved when we were getting the mail, that sort of thing."

"Vaida told me she'd done something...something that made her want to leave Dakota," Gavin told her. "Do you know what it was?"

She shook her head, tears filling her eyes again. "I'm sorry," she said softly, wiping her eyes with the back of her hand. "She was a nice girl. A sweet girl. I...she deserved better than to die somewhere where no one will ever miss her. But, I can't tell you what happened to her. Her story isn't mine to tell."

"She isn't here to tell it anymore," he said firmly.

"I'm afraid I can't help you. But, I know someone who might be able to," Joy said, eyes on the door as Gavin heard it open behind them. A woman entered, her long dark hair swinging down past her shoulders as she struggled with a large paper sack.

"Who are they?" the woman asked, staring at Gavin and Cody.

"Who is she?" Gavin asked.

"Hey, sweetheart, this is Fletcher and Cody. It seems we have some things to talk about."

"What?" Gavin and the woman asked at the same time. He spun around, staring at the knowing smile on Joy's face.

"Gavin, Cody, this is my sister, Sarah."

The woman stared at them. "What are they doing here?"

"Apparently they know Vaida Williams," she said, raising her eyebrows. "Apparently they were with her in Atlanta."

She squinted her eyes at her sister. "What? When?"

"For the past few months," Gavin answered.

"Apparently she died," Joy told her, her face pinched into a smile.

"Yeah, no kidding," Sarah said, not letting Gavin and Cody into their inside joke.

"What are we missing here?" Cody asked.

"Vaida Williams couldn't have been with you in Atlanta any time recently," Sarah told him plainly.

"What are you talking about?"

Joy looked at him, her face serious. "Boys, Vaida Williams has been dead for ten years."

TWENTY-SEVEN

GAVIN

Gavin stared at the women, sure he'd heard them wrong. "I'm sorry...what?"

"It's true," Sarah admitted. "She was our friend. But, she died years ago."

"I don't understand," Gavin told them, his heart pounding loudly in his ears. "She can't be dead. I mean, she is dead *now*. But, she wasn't. Not before. I was just with her."

Joy stood up, walking to a shelf and pulling an old red photo album from it. She flipped through the pages quickly, searching. When she landed on a page, she let out a loud 'ah-ha!' and held the book out to Gavin. "This is Vaida Williams."

He took the book from her grasp, settling it onto his lap and studying the picture. It was an old photograph, one that showed a younger Joy and Sarah with their wiry arms wrapped around a young black woman. She had her dark hair curled up around her face. From the way they were dressed, Gavin guessed the picture must've been from the early 2000s. There was something familiar about her smile, and yet, she was not the Vaida he knew.

He handed the book back. "It's not her," Cody confirmed.

"No," Joy said, "but I think I know who it was." She looked to Sarah, whose eyes were suddenly full of sorrow.

"No," Sarah said, touching her cheeks.

"I worry it's true." Joy nodded her head, walking to the window to look out. She moved the curtains away, looking through the blinds. "See, I told you when we saw him bring that car home that something was up. I knew it then."

"What is going on?" Gavin asked, moving to the window himself. "What car?"

Joy turned around, not giving him access to the window. "You should sit."

"Not until you tell me what's happening. If the girl I knew wasn't Vaida Williams, who was she? And why was she writing you letters?"

"Sit," Joy said again, more firmly this time. "We can help you. But only if you listen to what I have to say carefully. I raised two boys who are older than you; I know plenty about bull-headed men. I won't have you rushing out that door without all the information."

Gavin sat, seeing that she wasn't going to budge. "Fine. What information?"

"Joy, stop," Sarah said, her mouth tight. "You can't."

"What harm will it do now?" Joy asked, her voice cracking. "She's gone." Tears filled her eyes suddenly, and she looked away.

"It's not our secret to tell," Sarah said. "She wouldn't want us to."

"So, they just get no answers?" She shook her head. "They drove all this way to find out the truth; it's obvious they care about her."

"Cared," Sarah corrected. "Finding out the truth won't make it hurt any less."

"Can you just please tell us what's going on? I mean, we're sitting right here," Gavin said angrily. "And, if you don't tell us, we're going to keep digging. We won't give up at our first dead end." He didn't bother mentioning that this was just one of several dead ends they'd already hit. "So, you could save us a lot of trouble by just telling us what you know."

The women looked at him, then back at each other. Finally, Sarah sighed, sinking into the couch. Joy frowned, sitting down as well. "The girl you were with wasn't Vaida Williams, though it doesn't surprise me that that's the name she used."

"Makes sense," Sarah agreed quietly.

"Her name was Maggie. Maggie Harris," Joy said. "She was Vaida's granddaughter. They used to live in Chicago. It was where Maggie grew up. When Maggie was around nine or ten, her brother was shot and killed." Gavin gasped, but Joy went on. "It was...a really rough time for Maggie. Her parents had both died when she was very young, so Maggie and her siblings were left in Vaida's care. After Devon was killed, Vaida picked up and left the city, and they ended up here. It was just the three of them, Vaida, Maggie, and her baby sister, Danielle. That was when we met them. We'd keep the girls sometimes when Vaida worked. She was...strong. Stronger than she should've had to be. And tough on those girls, too."

"She just wanted them to be safe. She wanted to make sure they didn't end up like their parents...like their brother," Sarah explained.

"But, when Maggie got older, she rebelled. She met a boy." Her voice grew cold as she spoke, and Gavin was beginning to get an idea of where this story might be headed. "Riley Dereks." She rolled her eyes. "The boy was pure trouble. Vaida tried to keep Maggie from him, but she wouldn't listen. Snuck out, ran away, and got into trouble herself. By that time, Vaida was older. She struggled to do as much, and Maggie was relentless. She was nearly eighteen, and there was nothing anyone could do to stop her. So, Vaida gave in. She gave them her blessing, and they were married pretty quickly." She closed her eyes, touching her chest. "Vaida passed away a few months after their marriage. I don't know if Maggie ever forgave herself for it."

Sarah shook her head, dabbing her eyes as she listened to her sister talk. "Riley was to blame. Not Maggie. She was just a child."

"She knew what she was doing," Joy asserted. "Maggie wasn't innocent. She wasn't to blame for Vaida's death, but she wasn't innocent either."

"Either way," Sarah said, "Riley was a bad guy. *Is* a bad guy. I can't explain it, other than I knew she wasn't happy with him. Her light went out."

"Was he hurting her?" Gavin asked, feeling his face grow warm. His fists clenched without warning.

"We don't know for sure," Sarah said, looking to Joy.

"Maggie would never tell us, but after Vaida passed, we kind of took it upon ourselves to look after the girls. Danielle stayed with us for a while, in fact. Maggie was supposed to take care of her, but she was in no state to. We were the closest thing either of them had to family. Anyway, Riley was just...bad. Rude, controlling—abuse wouldn't surprise me in the least." New tears were in Joy's eyes as she went on. "He ruined her life. He ruined all of their lives."

"What happened to him?"

"Absolutely nothing," Joy said. "He got away with everything. And he'll get away with her death, too."

Gavin stopped, a breath stuck in his throat. Her words sent cold chills down his spine. "Her death? You think Riley killed her?"

"I know he did," she said.

"But, how could you?"

"A feeling. But more than that, her car's home. It's been gone for months, and it's back. How else would he have gotten it?"

"Her car?" Gavin asked, looking to the window. "That's the car you were talking about? You know where she lived?"

"They moved into Vaida's home after she passed away. It's directly across the street," Sarah answered.

He darted to the window, looking out at the house across the street. It was white with rusted metal siding and flower pots outside that were filled with rotten flowers. The yard was in need of mowing. It reminded him of the rundown house he'd once called home.

"That's her house?" he asked. His stomach knotted up at the mere thought of her.

"Was." Joy's face grew weary. "I'm afraid it'll go to Riley now."

"Vaida would be sick over it." Sarah clutched her stomach as if she, too, were going to be sick.

"Why would it go to him? He still lives there?" Suddenly it was all hitting him. "She was still *married* to him?"

"Yes," Joy said.

"What happened? Why was she in Atlanta?"

"We don't know," Sarah told him. "We'd been begging her for years to leave him. To get away before he killed her. But, we couldn't do much more than that. She was an adult, and it was her decision."

"So, you don't know why she left?"

"No. All we know is she disappeared. We worried like crazy. And then after a few weeks, we got a letter. No return address, but it was from Maggie. She said that she was safe and that she would be in touch as soon as she found a place where she knew he couldn't find her." She paused. "She wouldn't tell us anything else. Her phone was shut off."

"I think she was trying to protect us," Joy said. "In case Riley came to us wanting answers."

"And did he?"

"At first," Joy said. "He thought we'd stowed her away. But, he knew better than to threaten us. She wasn't here. We would've helped her if she'd come to us, and he knew that, but we would've never been stupid enough to let her stay here."

"We would've killed for her," Sarah said.

"Should have," Joy added.

"So, you really think Riley could've killed her? We should call the cops, then, right?"

"Go right ahead," Sarah said. "But it'll do you no good."

"Why's that?"

Just then, a knock sounded on the door, and they all grew still. "Who is it?" Joy asked Gavin.

He turned, looking out the window cautiously. Through the blinds, his vision was blurry, but his heart skipped a beat as he looked out onto the front porch. *No way.* It wasn't possible. And yet, there she was.

Unable to form words, he continued to stare at her, watching her as she glanced over her shoulder, her arms folded across her chest. Suddenly, his blood ran cold as he noticed what she was wearing.

No. No. No. He took a step back from the window, shaking his head. His mind was fuzzy, nothing making any sense. She'd lied to him. She'd lied to him about everything, and he was willing to forgive it all. But not this. He couldn't stomach it.

Sarah walked to the door, pulling it open. "Maggie?" she asked, her voice cracking as she disappeared behind the door to give her a hug. She pulled her in quickly, slamming it behind her.

Maggie's eyes, one black and bloody, grew wide as she saw him. Her bottom lip was swollen on the right side, and she parted them slightly. "Gavin?" she asked, not concealing his identity in her shocked state.

"Maggie," he said with a nod, not sure how to take this latest revelation. "When were you going to tell me you're a cop?"

TWENTY-EIGHT

VAIDA/MAGGIE
THE NIGHT SHE DISAPPEARED

Maggie screamed as the headlights swerved toward her, the red truck all too familiar. She took off running, her legs burning as she turned a corner. She could still hear the rumble of its engine behind her, a sound she'd had nightmares about every night since she left.

The headlights followed her, the truck on her tail. If only she could get to Gavin. Suddenly, she changed her course, running the opposite way. She couldn't go to Gavin. She couldn't put him in danger. If Riley got ahold of him, he'd kill him without thinking twice. She couldn't get him involved. If anything were to happen to him, she couldn't bear it.

Without warning, he stepped on the gas, swerving onto the sidewalk. She held her hands up to shield her face, sliding across the sidewalk as if she were running for home plate in a game of softball. A squeal escaped her throat as the car came to a stop, and she slid halfway underneath it.

She froze, breathing heavily, unable to believe she hadn't been crushed. She laid her head on the pavement as she caught her breath, knowing there was no way she'd make it away from him now.

The truck door opened and her husband stared down at her. "Hey there, Maggie," he said casually. "Sorry to cut your trip short. You always did look so cute when you run."

She sat up, crawling out from under the car and feeling the fear that she'd once grown so used to. "What are you doing here, Riley?"

"Don't you think that's a question I should be asking you?" He stepped down from the truck, bending over beside of where she sat. "Don't you know how worried about you I've been?" His hands went under her arms, lifting her up with force. She was tense in his grasp, waiting for the blows that would surely come. She considered her options: she could scream loudly and pray that someone would hear in time to save her, or she could allow him to take her. Either way, he would win. The streets were quiet so early in the morning during the week. If it had been a weekend, someone might've come along to help her. The streets were busier then. Or, she reminded herself, she might've gotten someone else hurt for her mistakes.

She allowed him to stand her up, her breathing erratic. "I'm...sorry," she whispered.

"Shhh," he told her, hugging her gently. "It's okay. It's all going to be okay. Let's just get you into the truck. We'll get you home where it's safe."

She nodded, allowing him to lift her up once again. He

put one arm under her legs, holding her like a baby, his warm breath on her face. "Come on, sweetheart," he said, placing her into the seat. "Climb across."

"Okay." She slid across the dirty seat, her eyes on the door handle. He put one hand on the seat, sliding onto it. When he shut the door, tears welled in her eyes. Her legs and back were bleeding from sliding across the pavement, but she hadn't noticed the pain until now. Her entire body was on high alert, just waiting for the snap.

He put the truck in reverse, and she watched his jaw tense. He checked his rearview, waiting as one or two cars drove past before he backed out. "Now, where do you live so we can go and get your stuff?"

She was silent, debating on what to tell him. What if he tried to hurt Cody? She couldn't risk it. THWACK. She blinked, her head slamming into the glass of the window as his elbow hit her jaw with force.

"I said where do you live?"

She could feel the blood dripping down her forehead but refused to move her hand to her skull. She wouldn't give him the satisfaction. She gave him the address, her voice dry and cracking.

"Good," he responded. "We'll just go and get your things, and then we can get you home. That's what you want, right?"

She looked down at her hands in her lap, picking at a piece of skin near her thumb. She nodded, her teeth grinding together.

"Good girl," he cooed.

She closed her eyes, wishing his truck would've just hit her. Whatever was waiting at home would be so much worse than that. His smell was making her nauseous. She'd hoped to never be so close to him again, but she'd gotten lazy. She never planned to stay in one place for this long. She should've left once she'd gotten the money from a few paychecks. Instead, she'd stayed. She'd stayed for a man she could never have. A man who made her feel safe when no one else could. A man who looked at her like she wasn't as damaged as she felt.

"Are you going to tell me why you left?" he asked.

"You know why," Vaida said angrily.

THWACK. Another elbow to the face. He slammed on the brakes, the tires screeching on the pavement so she was thrown forward, her face smacking the dashboard. "Excuse me?" he demanded. "Don't you get all high and fucking mighty with me, you stupid whore. You've moved to the big city, and suddenly you think you're invincible, huh?" He grabbed hold of her scalp, and though she tried to resist, he shoved it into the dashboard again. She tasted blood immediately, embarrassed by the tears that filled her eyes. They only seemed to make him angrier. "You make me like this. Don't you see that? It's you. I came here to make sure you were all right, and you force me to get angry."

She nodded. "I know."

He rubbed her head. "Why can't you just love me?" he asked. "I love you so much."

She winced at his touch, the blood from her busted lips seeping into her mouth. "I do," she lied. "I do love you."

"You don't!" he screamed. "You don't, or you wouldn't have left."

"I'm sorry," she said, feeling the tears coming again. She wiped them away, trying not to look at the blood that was on her palm.

"Are you?"

She nodded.

"You're never going to leave me again, are you?"

"No," she croaked, shaking her head. Her hands were trembling, though she hoped he wouldn't notice. "Never again."

"Good," he said. After a few moments, he spoke again, and she heard the edge in his voice that warned her worse was coming. "Who was the man you were with?"

"What man?" she asked simply, knowing that truth or lie, she would get the beating regardless. At least with a lie she could attempt to protect Gavin.

Surprisingly, he didn't hit her. Instead, he shook his head. "The man who got out of your car. The man who you went to Dale with."

She turned to look at him, shock taking her breath away. "You followed us?"

"I had an APB put out for your plate. My plate, really. The second you got close to home, I was alerted. I followed you to some puny funeral and watched you with...him. I thought you'd decided to come home to me, and instead you were off screwing some piece of shit."

"I wasn't—"

THWACK. "Don't lie to me," he roared, slamming his fist into her temple. Though he didn't have a good angle from her side, his force was still great. She let out a cry as her face hit the window again.

"Please," she begged. "Please...can we just forget it? I'm home now, I'm with you."

"You're so pathetic," he told her. "But, you know I'm not letting it go without a name. Lucky for you, I'll get the name without your help."

"What are you talking about?"

"Duke came with me. And he's following your little boyfriend home right now."

Duke. Riley's brother. "Riley," she begged. "Please. Please don't hurt him. He's not done anything wrong. Please, please." Panic began to set in as she realized she'd sentenced Gavin to his death.

"Don't worry, baby," he said, reaching toward her. She flinched, though he only slipped a hand around the back of her head and pulled her toward him. "We aren't going to hurt him yet. We're just going to figure out where he lives. Then, we'll run a check on his lease and find out his name. And then, if you ever run away again...I'll kill him." She gasped, choking back tears. "But we won't have to worry about that, will we?"

She shook her head. "No," she promised. "No. I'll never leave again."

"Good," he told her, sliding his arm around her shoulders and pulling her even closer with force. She scooted into the middle seat and shuddered as he kissed her cheek. "I don't know what I'd do without you."

She smiled stiffly, feeling bile rise in her throat. His hand tightened around her neck as he shoved her head into his lap. "Now, make yourself useful."

TWENTY-NINE

MAGGIE
BEFORE

"Maggie, hurry up," Riley called from the kitchen, his voice light.

"Coming," she called, grabbing the plates from the table and balancing them carefully on her arms. She hurried from the dining room toward the sink, placing the dishes in the sudsy water carefully. Riley hated when she made a mess.

"Want another beer, man?" Riley offered Noah.

"No, thanks," Noah said, tossing his beer into the trash. It bounced off and fell to the ground, shattering. "Oh, shit, dude. Sorry." He bent over to pick up the broken pieces.

"Get a rag, will you?" Riley asked Maggie, exasperation in his voice.

"Yeah, of course," Maggie responded, rushing to clean up the mess. She pulled Noah's hands back. "Let me."

"No," he said. "I've got it."

*"Just...*let me,*" Maggie said, knowing Riley was watching and making sure she didn't touch Noah's hands for too long. He stood up, facing Riley.*

"Well, we should get going," he said, wrapping an arm around Danielle.

"I was going to help Maggie with dishes," Danielle said.

"Maggie's got it," Riley said firmly, letting them know it wasn't up for discussion.

"Yeah, don't worry about it," she said, standing up with the broken shards lying on the white cloth. "It's not too much."

Her sister looked uneasy, but finally nodded. "I'll see you tomorrow, okay?"

Maggie nodded, searching for a box to put the broken glass in. She still had a scar on her leg from trying to take out a bag with broken glass in it from a few years ago. She remembered the way it felt, slicing her leg open, and refused to ever put glass in a trash bag again. Riley thought she was being paranoid.

She grabbed an empty beer box, tossing the shards in there, and then placed the box into the trash. It wasn't much protection, but hopefully it would do. She brushed off the front of her clothes, eyes on Riley as they led their guests to the living room. "I had a nice time," Maggie offered.

"Me too," Noah said. "Our place next time, right?"

"Mhm, you bet." Riley nodded, patting his friend on the shoulder.

Noah looked to Danielle. "Where's your purse?" he asked.

"Oh, it's in the kitchen. Just a sec," she said, walking out of the room. Riley's eyes followed her, and Maggie sensed his

agitation. He allowed her to have them over occasionally, but when the dinner was over, it was time for them to go. She knew he was growing more impatient the longer it took for the door to shut with them on the other side.

"How's Duke doing, Riley? I haven't seen him around."

"Eh, causing trouble like always, you know what I'm saying?" He laughed.

Noah grinned. "Sounds about like him. I don't see him around much anymore."

"He just got into the academy," Riley said with a grunt. "So, we'll see how that goes. Following in his baby brother's footsteps, I guess."

"Your dad must be proud," Noah said solemnly.

Riley let out a snort. "If he sticks with it, sure. He never sticks with nothing long, we both know that much. Some pretty long-legged thing will come around long enough to distract him, and he'll be off again." Noah nodded, the air growing tense around them. "Dani, you get lost in there?" Riley called, taking another swig of beer and heading toward the kitchen.

When he was out of earshot, Noah looked to Maggie. "You didn't have to clean up the beer bottle," he said, his voice low. "It was my mess."

"It was easier that way," she said, looking to the ground and tucking a piece of hair behind her ear.

"I don't like the way he treats you, Maggie," Noah said.

"Stop," she insisted, taking a step back as he reached for her arm. "You can't talk like that. He'll hear you."

"Maggie," he said, stepping toward her. "We can protect you from him. You know that, right? You don't have to be afraid of him."

For a moment, for one split second, Maggie heard his words. For just a second, she could fantasize about the life she could lead without Riley. Without fear. But, she shook her head. "No. Riley loves me. Just because he has a temper doesn't mean he doesn't love me."

"He controls you."

"He takes care of me," Maggie said, her hushed tone growing more angry. "Don't you dare pretend you know what's going on here. You have no idea what happens in my marriage."

"We worry about you," Noah said, his eyes locked on hers. Finally, he took a step back. "If you need a way out, you have it. That's all I'm saying."

"He's my husband," she said, wrapping her arms around herself.

"We're your family, too," he told her. "Your sister loves you. And I love her. I hate seeing her upset over you. I hate seeing you upset."

She shook her head. "You guys don't have to worry about me."

"What's going on?" Riley's voice called from behind them.

Maggie jumped, looking toward her husband with fear coursing through her. Noah took a step away from her. "Hey," he said. "I was just telling Maggie how good dinner was."

"She's a good cook," Riley agreed, though his voice had an edge to it that told her he didn't believe him.

Danielle appeared behind him, her purse in hand. "Sorry, guys. I had to run to the little girl's room. Are we ready?" she asked, looking between the three of them.

"Yeah," Maggie said, pulling open the door. "Goodnight, Dani." She didn't dare look at Noah.

"Goodnight," her sister said, rushing to her and giving her cheek a quick kiss. "Love you. See you."

Maggie was stiff as she mimicked the words back to her. She lowered her gaze as Noah tried to catch her eye. "Goodnight, Riley," he said finally, walking out the door behind his wife. Maggie shut the door, resting her hands against the wood and closing her eyes. She took a breath. "Well, that was—"

She inhaled sharply as she felt him grab a wad of her hair. He pulled the hair up so that she had to stand on her tiptoes to keep it from detaching at the root. She tried to hold in her cries. "What's wrong, sweetheart?" she asked, trying to turn so she could see his face.

He pulled it up higher, and she let out a cry. "I'm sorry," she said, reaching up to hold her head as he lowered it finally. He spun her around, his fingers still intertwined in her hair, and pressed his forehead into hers forcefully. There was a bit of spit in the corner of his mouth.

"What the fuck was that about?" he demanded, pressing his forehead into hers harder.

"I'm sorry," she said again.

"I leave you for two minutes, and you can't help flirting with your brother-in-law? For god's sake, Maggie. What kind of whore are you? Are you fucking him?"

"Of course not! I wasn't flirting, Riley, honest," she vowed. "We were just talking. He thanked me for dinner, that was it."

He flung her to the ground, and her body hit the carpet with a thud. "Do you think I'm stupid, you dumb bitch?"

"No," she cried, cowering on the floor. "No, of course not. You're smart, Riley. You're so much smarter than me."

"Are you making fun of me now?" he asked, bending over

her, spit flying as he screamed. She covered her stomach as he reeled his leg back, ready to kick. As the blows came, her mind shut off, allowing her to escape into the innermost crevices of her only safe place.

THIRTY

GAVIN

"When were you going to tell me you are a cop?" Gavin asked again, staring at the woman he thought he knew dressed in a police officer's uniform.

She shook her head. "I don't understand. What are you doing here?"

He ran a hand through his hair. "Making a huge mistake, apparently."

"I can't believe you're here. I never thought I'd see you again."

"Are you planning on turning me in?" he asked, his jaw tight. How could he have been so stupid? How could he have let himself trust his life-ending secret with someone he'd just met.

"What? No," she said, shaking her head. "You've got it all wrong. Can we talk? I want to tell you everything."

"It's too late for that. Vaida, you should have told me this.

I told you...I told you stuff that could ruin my life. And you couldn't tell me...you couldn't even tell me your name." He looked up at the ceiling, taking a breath.

"Gavin—"

"Who's Gavin?" Cody asked. "Why do you keep calling him Gavin?"

"*Fletcher*," she corrected. "I'm sorry. I have a lot on my mind. Fletcher, can we please talk? Alone?" Her eyes darted toward the hallway.

He remained still. "I don't think there's anything left to say." His heart ached as he stared at her, filled with both an undeniable need to run to her and a relentless fear screaming that he should run away.

"Please," she asked, rubbing a tear as it fell from her bruised eye. "Please. Just give me a chance to explain."

He thought for a moment, watching as another tear fell. How could he still care about her so much? How could watching her cry still cause him so much pain? "Fine," he agreed.

She breathed a sigh of relief, hurrying toward him. She made a move to touch his arm, but he pulled away even though there was nothing he wanted more than to touch her again. She held out an arm, leading him into the hallway and then into a small bedroom. "We'll be back," she told Joy, Sarah, and Cody as she shut the door.

"Take all the time you need, honey," Sarah said.

"Yeah, sure," Cody said sarcastically. "No need to include me in this secret meeting. I drove halfway across the state, too, you know."

Once the door was shut, Vaida stared at Gavin, her eyes soft. "It's so good to see you."

He nodded. "I'm glad you aren't dead."

She winced. "I'm sorry, Gavin. I'm so sorry."

"Sorry for what, Vaida? Sorry for risking my life by not telling me who you really are? Sorry for lying about it all even after I opened up to you? Sorry for breaking my heart the moment I heard that you'd died? Do you know how that felt?" Tears formed in his eyes. "I thought you were dead."

"I know," she said, reaching up and touching his arm carefully. He didn't pull away. "I'm sorry for all of it." Her eyes studied his, her lips parting. "My husband...he told you I died because he didn't want you to come looking for me. You or Cody. He didn't want you to ask any questions. I didn't give him your name. I didn't want you to be involved in this. I tried so hard to protect you. That's why I couldn't tell you who I was. I was trying to—"

"You didn't trust me," Gavin said. "That's why you couldn't tell me who you are. I told you the truth about my life, Vaida—Maggie. Whoever you are. I told you the truth about everything. But you couldn't trust me with your story."

"That's not it!" she cried, covering her mouth. "I do trust you. I do. I just couldn't risk you getting hurt."

"Well, it doesn't seem to matter now, does it? Because I'm hurt all the same."

"You aren't being fair," she told him.

"Fair?" he cried. "Fair? None of this is fair, Maggie. Life isn't fair. I could've helped you. I could've gotten you out of there. I could've gotten you away from him. I could've protected you. Instead, you've gone back to him, and I'm here looking like an idiot for chasing you across the state. And for believing every lie you've ever fed me. Including that you cared about me. Like you said, we were a mistake."

She closed her eyes. "Gavin, I do care about you. I'm sorry I lied. Please just listen."

"Why should I listen now? When I begged you before? I begged you to tell me the truth." The heartache, fear, and anger that radiated through him was bubbling out. He was sick of holding it in. Sick of holding everything in. For so long, he'd carried so many secrets on his shoulders alone. Finally with Vaida, er, Maggie, he felt like he could open up, but now he felt as though it had been done in vain.

"Because I was trying to keep you alive!" she screamed, her hands down to her sides in defeat.

"Alive?" he asked, feeling the weight of her words. "What do you mean?"

"Gavin, my husband is a mean man. A violent man. If he'd found you...if he had any reason to believe we had feelings for each other, he would've killed you. And he wouldn't have thought twice." Her voice was gravelly as she spoke.

"I can protect myself, Maggie. You don't have to—"

"That's what they all think, Gavin. I couldn't chance it with you. I couldn't...I couldn't stand to risk losing you. It would've killed me." She began sobbing, though she spoke through her sobs. "I'm sorry I lied to you. I wanted to tell you everything. I wanted to tell you every single secret, and I wanted to feel like we could make it through together. But, I didn't want you to know what I'd done. I didn't want you to see this ugly side of me."

"Can't you see that I don't care?" He reached for her without thinking, and she fell into his arms. "I'm crazy about you, Maggie. I would've done anything for you. I don't care what you've done or who you were. I don't care what kind of danger it puts me in...feeling this way. All I care about is that you're safe. And that you know I'm going to be here for you. If you let me. But, I can't stand secrets. I can't handle them. You have to trust me. Wholly. Like I trust you."

She nodded, her face moving against his shirt. "I just really have trouble trusting anyone. The last time I trusted a man he destroyed me. My life, my mind, everything about who I was or ever hoped to be...he stole it. So trust doesn't come easy for me. Especially not to men."

"I am nothing like your husband, Maggie. I would never do anything to hurt you."

"I see that now," she said. "But he promised that once, too." She looked up to stare at him, and he ran a finger over her bruise.

"You ran away from him?"

She nodded. "Not far enough."

"How did he find you?"

She lowered her head. "It doesn't matter, Gavin. The point is that he did."

"It matters to me."

"He saw us when we came home. To your mother's funeral."

Gavin froze, his chest pounding. "This is my fault?"

"No," she said, squeezing his shoulders with her hands and staring at him. Her voice was firm when she spoke again. "Listen to me," she said, following his eyes as they moved and commanding them to lock with her own. "This was not your fault. None of this. I should've gotten a new car as soon as I came to town. I should've left town after I got my first paycheck. There are a number of things that led up to him finding me, but none of it boils down to you. It's me. I was careless and reckless and stupid."

"You aren't stupid," he said.

"You don't know everything. I am...the things I've done, the people I've hurt," she said, wiping her eyes with shaking hands. "When I said I was a monster, I wasn't exaggerating or being dramatic. It's the truth—one of the only true things I could tell you."

"Maggie, stop," Gavin said, caressing her cheeks with his thumb. "My past is far from pretty. I'm a criminal who's on the run. No one even knows my name. No one except you. How could I ever judge you for anything when my life is one big mess? I don't care what you've done. I only care about who you are now."

She hung her head to the side, staring at him with a haunted expression. "What if I don't know who I am anymore?"

He pulled her into him again, kissing her forehead. "We can figure it out together. As long as you don't shut me out."

She nodded, lifting her chin up and pressing her mouth onto his. Her lips quivered as cool tears touched his skin. Their kiss was gentle and cautious, Gavin's hands around her hips.

"Whatever you need," he told her when she pulled away, "we can make it happen together. I won't push. I understand your fears, but if we do this, if we really do this...we have to be in it together. You have to be honest with me at all times. There are too many secrets in our lives, both of us could be at risk if we aren't honest."

She nodded. "Okay."

"Where is your husband now?" Gavin asked finally. "We need to get you far away from this town. We can take Cody's car. We'll figure out how to get a new one somewhere else."

"We can't go back to Atlanta, Gavin."

"I know," he agreed. "He knows where I live. He knows where you lived."

"No," she said, placing her head onto his shoulder, her breath warm against his skin. "It's not about him. It's about me. I can't face that town anymore. I'm sorry. I know it's your home. I know you love your life there, but I just...I cant. After he found me, after he beat me, he tied me up in his truck and drove to the apartment. He loaded up my stuff in the car and had his brother drive it back. I remember sitting in the floorboard while he was outside of your apartment, knowing what he was telling you, knowing how you would feel. I just...I can't—"

"So, we don't go back," Gavin said. "I've started over plenty of times, Maggie. Th—"

"Vaida," she corrected. "I want to be Vaida. Maggie is someone I'd rather leave behind."

He nodded, kissing her forehead over a deep wound. "Vaida, then. I've started over so many times. New places, new people...that's fine with me. As long as you're with me, I don't feel so alone."

"Gavin, I...there's one more thing you need to know before you make any decisions about me."

"Okay," he said. "What is it?"

She closed her eyes, placing her palms over them as more sobs tore from her throat. She sank to the floor, her mouth open as the cries grew louder. He sat down on his knees, holding her in his arms and rocking, allowing her to work through what she needed to. He kissed her head, moving the hair back from her face and waiting until she had calmed down.

When her cries had quieted, she leaned away from him, tear stains down her cheeks. "You know, I used to love being a cop." He nodded, and she went on. "My dad was an officer in Chicago, and I guess it was my way of paying tribute to him. I don't know if that makes any sense. Anyway, Riley's dad is the town sheriff, and he got him into the academy before we got married. Then, when he graduated, his dad helped me get in." She shook her head. "I always thought it would make me feel powerful, like I was making some sort of difference, but Riley never let that happen. I was never allowed to do anything worthwhile. I couldn't have a partner he didn't approve of...and he didn't approve of any of them. So, I left the force. It was the hardest thing I've ever done. He wanted me at home, and so that's where I went. The dutiful wife," she said with a sneer. "But, today, I put on the uniform again. Not because it matters. Not because I'm getting back on the force, but because it was the only way I could feel close to my parents again. I came over here to say goodbye to Joy and Sarah, because besides my sister, they're the only family I have left. And then, I was going to turn myself in."

"Turn yourself in? For what?" he asked, shocked by her words.

She swallowed hard.

"Vaida, what did you do?" he asked again.

No tears fell from her eyes as she said the words that caused his throat to go dry. "I killed my husband."

THIRTY-ONE

MAGGIE
BEFORE

The next morning, Maggie was scrubbing the kitchen sink, making sure the house was extra clean for Riley. She didn't need anything else to set him off. A knock on the door caused her to jump, and she rushed toward the living room. Had he forgotten his keys? She swung open the door, her heart sinking at the sight of the face waiting for her.

"Noah, you can't be here," she said through the storm door.

"Oh my god," he said, seeing her neck, the fingerprints she'd tried desperately to cover. "Maggie." His face went white as he stared at her.

"I'm fine, Noah, honestly. You should go. If he sees you here, it'll just be worse."

"I'm not leaving," he said firmly. "Let me in, or so help me god I'll—"

"You'll what Noah?" she asked, trying to hold in her tears.

"You'll go to the police?" He swallowed hard, seeming to only then realize that wouldn't be a choice. "You can't protect me. No one can."

"I'm not leaving," he said again. "Come with me. Right now. I will find a way to keep you safe. I promise you that. You don't have to live like this, Maggie."

"Who said anything about living?" she asked, lowering her gaze. "I'm lucky just to be surviving."

"You are better than this," he told her. "Why would you stay with him?"

"Don't you get it, Noah? This is what I deserve. This is my punishment." The words that filled her head every day escaped her throat before she could stop them.

"Your punishment? For what? What are you talking about?"

"For Vaida. For our grandmother. When I left home to be with Riley, so sure that I was right and she was crazy about him, she was so sick...she didn't survive it. Couldn't. I killed her, Noah—"

"No, you didn't," he tried to argue.

"I did," she said louder. "I did. Not outright, no, but it's my fault she's dead. After everything she did for me...I betrayed her."

"You were seventeen. You were just a kid."

"I was a brat," she said simply. "And it cost my grandmother everything, up until she had nothing left to give. She was depressed and sick...and I didn't have the decency to take notice or care."

"You don't deserve this," Noah reiterated. "Vaida wouldn't have wanted this."

"I never cared what she wanted when it counted."

"Maggie, please...let me help you."

Just then, the sound of Riley's truck roared into the neighborhood. She glanced at the clock, he shouldn't be home for a few more hours, but the rumble was unmistakable. Her eyes grew wide, trying to decide whether to pull Noah into the house to hide him or leave him outside to be found. She didn't know which would be worse.

In the end, she made a mistake that had haunted her every day since. "Get in here," she cried, opening the door and pulling him inside just as the truck rounded the corner. She said a silent thank you for the warning of his truck, not sure why he had decided to leave his squad car at the station so often. She shut the door quickly, shoving Noah toward the back of the house. "You have to go," she cried. "Get out of here before he sees you."

"Maggie, come with me," he said, stopping and grabbing her hands.

"I can't," she said in a hurried whisper, her heart thudding loudly in her chest. "Noah, you have to get out of here. He'll kill us both."

"He's going to see my car outside," he warned her, and the truth of his statement took her breath away.

"I'll think of something. Please just go," she begged. He nodded, seeing the fear in her eyes, and darted for the laundry room, trying to open the old wooden windows. He shoved with all of his might, groaning.

"Shh," she shushed him just as the front door opened. She heard Riley's heavy footsteps.

"Maggie, where are you?" His voice boomed through the house, making her gulp. She took a deep breath, letting it out slowly as she tried to quiet her racing heart.

"I'm in here," she called, hurrying out of the laundry room and shutting the wooden door behind her. The old, white paint was beginning to crack, and she couldn't help but picture it cracking more as it tried to conceal the giant secret that lay behind it. The secret that could ruin everything.

Riley was standing in the kitchen with a bottle of wine and a bouquet of flowers. She smiled at him, taking the flowers graciously. "What's Noah's car doing outside?" he asked.

"Someone was blocking Joy and Sarah's driveway earlier," she lied. "He asked to park in front of the house. What are these for?" she asked, changing the subject.

He kissed her lips, seeming to accept that answer. "Just because," he whispered.

She wrapped her arms around his neck, kissing him deeper and trying to keep him distracted. He ran the wine bottle down her back, the cool glass chilling her through her shirt. She pulled away, taking the bottle and setting it and the flowers on the counter.

"You're so sweet," she said, grabbing his hand and pulling him toward the bedroom.

He stopped. "Don't you want to put the flowers in some water?"

She shook her head, trying to keep her panic at bay as she heard a noise from the laundry room. She prayed he hadn't heard it as well. "I will," she said with a fake smile, "but I want you first."

He shook his head. "Naughty girl." Another knock came from the laundry room, this time loud and undeniable. "Did you hear that?" he asked.

Fear coursed through her veins as she tried to keep her voice steady. "I didn't hear anything, babe."

He narrowed his eyes at her and pointed to the door. "It's coming from in there."

She shook her head, grasping his shirt and pulling him into a kiss. "I don't hear anything, Riley." She ran her hands over his ears. "But I do feel something." Her hands traveled down his legs, making their way to his zipper.

He pulled her hands off of him quickly. "What the hell are you hiding?" He darted across the room and shoved open the door with a quick turn of the knob. Maggie held her breath as he walked in, looking around. To her surprise, Noah was no longer in the room. He took another step further into the room, and suddenly the door swung shut and she heard Riley groan, let out a scream, and then there was a thud.

She pushed open the door, gasping as she stared at Noah. He held the iron in his hand, his chest panting heavily. "Maggie, run!" he told her.

"What did you do?" she asked, a hand over her mouth as she stared at her husband's body on the floor.

"He's not dead," Noah said. "Just knocked out." He dropped the iron, grabbing hold of her hand and pulling her from the room. "We have to go before he wakes up."

"I...I can't," she said. "I have to make sure he's okay."

"Maggie," Noah said firmly. "He will kill you. If not today, eventually. I can't let that happen. I can't watch Danielle lose you. I won't."

Maggie shook her head. "I can't just leave him."

He grabbed hold of her shoulders. "You have to," he told her. "You have to leave him, Maggie. We have to run."

Her brain began to get fuzzy as she felt tears forming in

her eyes. A scream ripped from her throat, and she suddenly felt as though she couldn't catch her breath. A weight filled her chest as she sank to the ground, trying desperately to find oxygen. What was happening? She couldn't breathe, couldn't think. She covered her eyes, the darkness calming her only slightly. A hand touched her back, his fingers rubbing her shoulders. Her ears ringing and her body growing numb, she looked up, sure she was going to pass out at any moment.

Something moved to their right, and her gaze flicked from Noah to the laundry room as Riley stood up. She tried to scream, to warn Noah as Riley pulled his gun from his holster, but no sound could be formed. She watched helplessly as Noah tried to stand her up and the sound of the bullet ripped through the house. Noah never even looked his way, his life ending before the sound could even register to him as dangerous. He fell to the ground, the back of his head splattered across their white carpet. Maggie felt the contents of her stomach as they bubbled in her belly, spewing forcefully out of her mouth. She fell to the ground, her eyes locked with Noah's empty ones. And then, it all went black.

WHEN VAIDA WOKE UP, *Noah's body was gone. She blinked heavily, staring around the room. She didn't dare move, not wanting to alert Riley that she had woken up.*

She shut her eyes quickly as she heard his voice. "Yeah," he said firmly. "I'll talk to you soon. Gotta go."

He slammed the phone down onto a hard surface, probably the table, and walked toward her. Her heart was pounding as she tried to lay completely still. His boot shoved into her kidneys. "Get up," he growled. She would never know if he knew she was awake or if it was just lucky timing. Her eyes shot open, hands on her back.

"Ow," she croaked. He kicked her again where her hands rested, and she felt her finger pop. She prayed it wasn't broken. The last time he'd broken her finger had been unbearable, and she wasn't sure she could handle it again.

"I said get up,*" he bellowed, grabbing hold of her arm and lifting her into the air so she squealed, sure her arm was going to snap out of its socket. He swung her around, grabbing her jaw with one hand and squeezing her cheeks so her lips poked out. "You're a damn liar, my dear wife. What was he doing here?" he demanded, his face not an inch from hers.*

She couldn't speak, her stomach still rumbling from the smell of blood that permeated the air.

He turned her head quickly, forcing her to look at the blood-soaked carpet. "Look what you did, you stupid whore." He pressed his lips into her ear, his teeth on her lobe. She squeezed her eyes shut, unable to look, which only made him angrier. He shook her face in his hand. "Don't you close your fucking eyes."

She opened them, staring at the blood as the bile rose in her throat. "He didn't do anything wrong," she choked out, hot tears falling down her cheeks.

"Excuse me?" he screamed, throwing her to the ground and straddling her stomach. He pressed his hand over her mouth and pushed down with all of his might. It felt like her teeth were going to break off, the force enough to cause her lips to start bleeding. "He attacked me in my own house. He was seeing my wife behind my back. What the hell do you mean he didn't do anything wrong?"

She shook her head, unable to speak to defend him. Riley pressed down harder. "I love you," he said to her. "Don't you see that? Don't you see how much I love you? I killed for you, Maggie. I killed to keep you mine forever. I couldn't bear to lose you." He pressed his nose into hers, moving his hand to kiss her lips. In that moment, fire filled her belly. She gave in to his kiss, and when she felt his tongue enter her mouth, she bit down as hard as she could. He tried to pull away, but was unable to move far. His fist pounded against her skull and she released him. He reached for his mouth, and she slid out from under him quickly, making a run for it.

He yelled after her, cursing loudly. She ran through the living room, into the dining room with him on her tail. He knocked over a chair and launched another one in her direction. It narrowly missed her, slamming into the wall and knocking a shelf down. Glass from her grandmother's knickknacks and the few pictures they owned went everywhere. She slid into the bedroom, trying to shut the door as his fingers shoved into the threshold to stop it from latching.

"I don't think so," he cried, pushing back against it. She was filled with every emotion, and it was pure adrenaline that allowed her to match his strength, her feet sliding against the carpet. She looked for a weapon, but there was nothing within reach. If she let go of the door, he would kill her. There was no doubt in her mind. He would kill her like he'd killed Noah. Without one second thought. She stared at the window; could she jump through it? The glass would hurt her, but it wouldn't kill her. Most likely, anyway. She let go of the door, her bare feet digging into the carpet as she ran toward the window at breakneck speed. She launched herself into the air, covering her eyes, and was jerked back instantly. He had

ahold of her hair, and then her neck. He grabbed her, throwing her over his shoulder and slamming her into the wall.

She cried, accepting her defeat as he walked back to the living room without a word. How would he do it? Would he shoot her? That would be preferable. Would he beat her until she could no longer breathe? Break another rib like he had before? She hoped he wouldn't drown her. He knew that was her worst fear, but had yet to try it.

She closed her eyes as he threw her onto the floor. "That was a stupid choice, Maggie," he told her, shaking his head as he rubbed his jaw. "It didn't have to be like this."

She didn't respond, curling up into a ball and trying to tune out his words. She awaited her fate; she was ready for it to be over. Finally, he leaned down, shoving her face into the carpet so she could taste Noah's blood. "I'm going to go get a bucket. You're going to clean up this mess," he said. "And then I'll decide what to do with you." He started to walk away but stopped. "If you so much as move a goddamn muscle, I will shoot you where you stand. And then I'll go shoot your dumbass sister, too."

His words chilled her to the core, the truth in them evident. She nodded, unable to meet his eyes as he walked into the kitchen. She looked around the room, but there was nothing. No way out and nothing to protect herself with. He was back within seconds, anyway. He tossed a soapy sponge at her and set down a bowl of water. "Get to cleaning. I don't want anything left."

She nodded, getting on her hands and knees and realizing how sore she really was. The adrenaline had kept her from feeling it until that moment. She worked the soap into the carpet, scrubbing the blood, though it was merely moving the stain around rather than cleaning it up.

"What did you do with his body?" she asked.

From where he sat, Riley stared at her, hatred in his eyes. "Ask me any more questions and you'll get to see firsthand."

She closed her eyes. "I'm trying to protect you. You can't bury him close to the house."

He stood, rubbing his chin, one hand on the gun in his holster. "Protecting me, huh?" he asked.

"Yes."

"Like you were protecting him earlier? Is that right? This is all your fault, Maggie. All of it. If you weren't such a whore, none of us would be in this mess. He's dead because of you."

She nodded. "I know."

He seemed surprised by her response. "So, you admit it?"

"Yes," she said. "I'm sorry, Riley. I'm so sorry. I messed up. It's all my fault." Fresh tears began to fall from her eyes, and he leaned down next to her. He didn't make a move to wipe them up, but some of the anger seemed to fade.

"Stand up," he told her.

"I need to clean up the rest of—"

"I said stand up." She did as she was told, the sponge still in her hand. "Now, tell me what he was doing here."

"He...he wanted to check on me after last night."

"Check on you why?"

She shook her head. "He knew you were mad. He was just...he was being nosy. About us. About me."

"He always liked you. I knew that, even in school. He married Danielle just to get close to you."

She nodded, doing whatever it took to appease him. "You're right, baby. He just wanted me. But, I never wanted him. You're it for me, Riley." She didn't dare lean in, studying his face to see if he was buying it. His expression was stony for a moment, but then it softened.

"You're mine."

"I'm yours," she reiterated.

"I'll kill anyone who ever touches you."

"No one ever will again," she promised.

He took a step toward her, his hand moving away from his gun and onto her hips. "Why would you try to hurt me?" he asked.

"I'm sorry," she said, kissing his lips. "I was scared. And confused."

"You could've ripped my tongue off."

"I'd never do that," she said. "I like your tongue." She kissed him deeper, her hands around his neck. He pulled her to him, running his hands through her hair. She felt the tension leave his shoulders as the argument finally seemed to be over. She kissed his neck, trying not to let him feel the way she was shaking or the tears that were cascading down her cheeks.

Lord, forgive me, *she said a silent prayer as she reached for his belt buckle, letting his pants fall to the floor. He pushed her onto her knees and she went down without a fight. They locked eyes as she wrapped her lips around him, his expression filling with fire. He looked up at the ceiling, letting out a groan. Seeing her chance, she moved her hands quickly to his holster, grabbing the gun. He looked down, realizing what was happening as she backed up and pointed the gun in his direction. He lunged for her, and she pulled the trigger.*

The deafening sound tore through the house again, and he crumpled to the floor.

THIRTY-TWO

MAGGIE
AFTER

On the way back to Dakota from Atlanta, Riley didn't talk much. He kept Maggie's hands and feet bound and only untied her when they stopped once to allow her to use the bathroom.

Maggie knew better than to fight back this time. He wouldn't let his guard down around her again, not when she'd tried to kill him before her big escape. Thought she had killed him, in fact, though she had been too afraid to check. The fear that he was still alive was always there in the back of her mind. Her shot had been off. She'd jumped as she pulled the trigger, and he'd moved toward her. Blood covered his back so quickly she couldn't be sure where she'd hit him, and she didn't dare check.

And now she was paying for that. He'd take her back to their home and murder her. And then she'd end up wherever

Noah's rotting corpse was. Would Danielle's body already be there? She teared up at the thought. It would be her fault. All her fault. There were so many deaths on her conscience already. She shook her head, not allowing herself to think about it anymore. She didn't have time to break down right now.

When they finally pulled into the driveway, the sight of the house gave her a familiar ache in her heart. A place that had once brought her so much joy was now the symbol of so much grief. He pulled her from the car, an arm around her waist so it looked as though they were just walking together as husband and wife, rather than captor and prisoner.

He shoved her into the house, a chair in the middle of the floor waiting for her. He sat her in it, tying her down. She didn't resist.

"What are you going to do to me?" she asked.

"Whatever I want," he said casually, standing up as he finished the tie.

She hung her head. "Just kill me, Riley."

"What?" he asked, staring down at her.

"Just...just get it over with. It's what you're going to do anyway."

"I don't want you dead, Maggie. Or...should I say Vaida?"

"Don't say her name," she spat.

"Vaida, Vaida, Vaida," he said with a cackle. "I don't want you dead. I want you to be with me. I want you to stop running. You're the only one who gets me. But, until you love me the right way...I'm going to keep you here. Until you calm down. I can't risk you running off again. I can't risk you going back to anyone else."

"Anyone else? What does that mean?"

"I saw you at the funeral, Maggie. I saw you with that man you claimed you work with. I can't let that happen again."

"Meaning what?"

"Meaning I'm going to take care of him so you no longer have that option. Meaning I'm going to take care of every option you ever have until you realize I'm the only one who can love you the right way."

"What are you talking about?" she asked, feeling sick. "You're going to kill him? Riley, please don't. Please," she begged, struggling against her ties. What if he already had? "You don't have to do that. I do love you. I do. I know you're the right guy for me."

"Enough," he silenced her. "We all know you deserve an Oscar, *Maggs. You don't have to convince me. Besides, I'm not in the killing mood. Not today, anyway. But, I am going to make sure you never see him again."*

"I won't ever see him," she promised. "You don't have to worry about that."

"I know I don't," he told her. "Because he's going to be locked up for a very long time."

"What?" she said, very little power behind her voice as her skin grew cold.

He sat down across from her, an evil grin on his face. "See, I'm betting you don't know much about the man you were with, but he's a bad guy, Maggie. A criminal." He shook his head as if she hadn't watched him shoot a guy's face off just a few months ago. "He lied to you about who he is."

"What are you talking about?"

His face grew strange. "Or...maybe he didn't." He stood again, giving her a shrug. "Maybe he told you that he is a criminal on the run. That he killed his father in a fire. That his own mother was so terrified of him she couldn't tell the truth until she was on her deathbed." He pulled a cigarette from his shirt pocket and lit it, letting the smoke set in his lungs before he breathed it out through his nose. "And see, you led us right to him. You're a hero, Maggs. We would've never found him if you hadn't come back into town. And to the mother's funeral. Then, after, I followed you both to his brother's house. And that's when I began to piece it all together. My father had heard all about the missing twins, the killer twins...and he'll be all too thrilled when I tell him exactly where he can send the cops to pick one of them up. Hell, maybe there's even a reward. We can live well, all because your little boyfriend is a killer—"

"No, please! Please don't do this, Riley!" she screamed, struggling with her ties and bouncing the chair against the ground until it fell over. She lay on the floor, crying loudly and feeling more helpless than ever. "You don't have to do this. Please. You don't have to." Tears rolled out of her eyes and into her hair, her face resting on the carpet. The ties were pinching her as she lay on the floor, but she couldn't focus on that. She'd never survive someone else, anyone else, dying because of her. But certainly not Gavin.

"Oh, I know I don't have to," Riley said, walking out of the room. "I just want to."

RILEY DIDN'T LET *her eat anything the rest of the day, and he kept her tied to the chair except when he moved her to the bed to rape her. It seemed like he had a newfound sex drive since she'd been gone. She didn't fight it—his bony body on top of her—didn't open her eyes no matter how many times he slapped her. She just prayed it would end. Prayed it would all be over soon.*

Mostly, she slept. Hoping she wouldn't have to wake up. At one point, she awoke to hear another woman's voice. Her eyes fluttered open carefully as she tried to focus on it.

He had moved the chair into the bedroom, and she was listening through the closed door.

"I know, baby," Riley was saying. "It won't be too long. I promise you it won't."

"I just want you to myself," the voice said. It was a voice she recognized. A voice that should've made her feel relieved to hear it, but instead made her sick.

"You'll have me soon enough," Riley responded, and then there was kissing. She could hear the panting and moaning as their kisses grew hot and heavy. Riley had always been a loud kisser.

"Where will we go?" Danielle asked. "We can't stay here. I don't want to live any place where you have so many memories with her."

"We can go wherever you want," Riley promised. "You name it, and we'll be there. After they left us, we deserve happiness, right?"

"You're the only one who understands," she said, her voice muffled. "I don't know how I'd get through this without you." She let out a laugh then, and Maggie heard them kissing once more.

Maggie almost called out to her as she heard the words, hopeful that her sister may have only turned to Riley in a moment of need.

"Good riddance," Riley said, and Maggie stopped before she began to scream. "I was getting tired of having to hide you anyway."

"I know," Danielle agreed. "Although, secret sex was a lot of fun." More kissing. Maggie squeezed her eyes shut, wishing she could cover her ears as the kisses grew more passionate and the moans grew more lustful. She heard her sister's panting, Riley's grunts, and the unmistakable sound of the kitchen table scooting across the floor.

She rolled her eyes, feeling more helpless than ever. Danielle had been distant since their grandmother passed, but she would've never believed she could be sleeping with Riley. Not that she was jealous. God, she could have him. But then again, she'd never wish that fate on anyone. If only Danielle could know the truth about Noah. But, if she tried to get her attention, Riley might kill her, too. Mad at her as she currently was, she couldn't bear for him to kill anyone else. Couldn't bear to deal with anyone else's death. Not Gavin's, and especially not Danielle's.

She closed her eyes again, hoping sleep would find her quickly. She had to come up with a plan. No longer was waiting for death an option. She needed to save Gavin. Warn him of what was coming. And she couldn't do that if she was playing some pitiful damsel in distress. It was time to channel her inner-Vaida.

THIRTY-THREE

MAGGIE
AFTER

Maggie had gone all-out mad woman waiting for Riley to come back into the room. Over the past few hours, she had managed to stay silent as she broke both of her thumbs in order to escape her handcuffs, a little trick she'd learned from a criminal in her first week of duty. It hurt, oh god it hurt, but she was focused. She was getting out. She had to. Gavin's life depended on it.

Once her hands were free, she'd untied her feet and then began working to break off a piece of long spindling wood from the back of the chair to use as a weapon. Now she just had to wait. She had listened carefully to him stomping around the house all morning. Danielle had left very early.

Finally, she'd heard him coming, his pounding footsteps echoing down the hall. She braced herself, the chair in her hands. As soon as the door swung open, she launched the chair at him, its heavy wood connecting with his head. He ducked, covering the spot that immediately split open on his forehead. He stared at her with wild eyes, and she knew this was it. Her or him. Only one could leave the room alive.

As he lunged for her, she pushed off the ground, the wood from the chair's back held firmly in her hand. They smacked into each other, falling to the floor. He was on top of her, his hand around hers, trying desperately to pry the makeshift weapon out of her fingers. She squeezed tighter, pressing her feet into the carpet and trying desperately to scoot away from him. She felt herself move an inch, just enough for him to let go, trying to reposition himself, and she swung. The wood connected with his chest, and he shot back, a shocked expression on his face. She swung again, and again, and again, as the wood began penetrating his skin. He fell back, cursing and sputtering as blood began to soak his shirt and the floor underneath him. Rage filled her, and she continued to stab him, screams ripping from her chest as blood pooled in his mouth.

This time she didn't run away. She waited. She watched. She made sure he was gone. Dead. Never to threaten her or anyone else again. When the light left his eyes and his last haggard breath escaped his chest, she stood, dusting off her knees and walking from the room.

THIRTY-FOUR

GAVIN

Gavin listened as she told her story—the whole, horrible thing—her eyes haunted and sentences choppy in between her sobs. When she was finished, she collapsed in his arms, letting him hold her until her cries had slowed down enough for her to catch her breath.

He took her hands in his, staring at the dark, swollen skin around her thumbs. She moved to pull them away, but he kissed them carefully. "You did all of that for me," he said, the only words he could muster without breaking down himself. If the man hadn't already been dead, he would've been after Gavin was done with him. His insides were a boiling pit of rage as he stared at the strong woman he'd grown to know looking so full of fear.

"I'm no hero, Gavin. I was protecting you after I got you into a mess. I've hurt so many people."

"It wasn't your fault," he said firmly.

"Yes, it was. Noah would've never—"

"No," Gavin interrupted. "If there's one thing I've come to accept after everything that's happened to me, it's that what *they* did to us, it's their guilt to carry, even if they never will. You made the most of the cards you were dealt, and that caused you to have to make horrible decisions...but you are not responsible for what happened. Not to you or Noah, Riley or me, or anyone. You did what you had to do, Vaida. You aren't a monster. You're a survivor."

She shook her head. "How is it you can look at me like that after all I've told you?"

"Because nothing has changed. In fact, I'm even more into you now, if that's possible."

"What?" she asked, looking at him as if he were crazy.

"Look, if anyone can understand your shitstorm of a life, it's me. I can relate to you in a way no one else ever could. And, when I look at you all I see is strength. You were brave in a situation that no one should ever have to go through. You didn't just give in. You fought back. And you won. You got out, Vaida. That's what matters. You got out without anyone's help. You didn't need saving. You were brave enough, smart enough, strong enough to save yourself. That doesn't make you a monster, it makes you—" He paused, his eyes lighting up. "I want to be a total guy right now and say sexy, but I'll go with admirable, instead."

She smirked. "I never thought anyone could look at me and see strength. Not after he called me weak all those years."

"You're the strongest person I've ever met," he told her honestly, brushing a piece of hair back from her eyes and tucking it behind her ear. "I'm so in awe of you."

She surprised him by letting out a small laugh. "What kind of messed up are we?"

He pulled her to him, their lips only inches apart. "The very best kind." She lifted her lips to meet his, their kiss soft. He put a hand on her cheek, careful of her bruises. The world was suddenly frozen around them, and nothing else seemed to matter as Gavin's pulse sped up. She ran her hands over his stubble, locking her fingers together behind his neck.

"I think I'm falling for you," she said when they broke apart, both breathing heavily.

"Join the club," he told her, rubbing his nose over hers.

"Really?"

"More than you know," he said, kissing her again."Now, we need a plan. You don't want to go back to Atlanta. I say we head to New York and get your fake ID. Then we can go anywhere you want."

She nodded. "The police will be looking for me. Once news gets out that Riley is dead. His dad won't give up. He may just be a small town sheriff, but he's powerful. He won't stop looking for me."

Gavin stood and walked to look out the window, trying to think of where they'd be the safest when a crazy idea came to him. "What if they don't know he's dead?"

"Huh?"

"What if you both just went...missing?" he asked.

"I'm lost," she told him. "And, just to clarify, I mean that in the *I don't understand you* sort of way, not the *I'm missing* way."

He grinned at her joke. "I have a plan. It's totally insane. And we'll have to tell one other person your secret.

But, if we can pull it off, it'll mean we'll both be a lot safer."

"Do you trust this person?"

"With my life," he said without hesitation. "But more than that, with yours."

THIRTY-FIVE

GAVIN

Gunner arrived at Sarah and Joy's house two hours later, looking serious. He climbed out of his car, meeting Gavin at the door.

"What's going on?" he asked.

"Did you bring the stuff?"

Gunner nodded. "Gavin, what happened?"

"It's complicated," he said. "But, I need your help."

"You know I'll do anything I can to help you," Gunner said, placing a hand on his brother's shoulder.

"How much do you remember about cleaning up a crime scene?" Gavin asked, wincing.

"It's like riding a bike, right?" Gunner joked, a worried look on his face. "But, from the look on your face, I'm assuming I'm not going in after the cops?"

Gavin shook his head. "It's Vaida's ex-husband. He...how much do you want to know?" he asked.

"Whatever I need to."

"Long story short, he was an abusive asshole. And, now he's dead." He left out whether Vaida or he himself was responsible for that. "But, we need to make sure no one knows it. We need to...the body is still..."

Gunner nodded, seeming to understand.

"I know I'm asking you to commit a crime, so if you don't want to do it, if you can just teach me...I'll take care of it. You have a family. I don't blame you if you can't incriminate yourself."

"I do have a family," Gunner said. "And you're a part of that. Besides, I was really good at my old job. But, I could use the help if you want to learn how." He smiled. "It'll be like Take-Your-Brother-To-Work-Day."

Gavin shook his head. "When did you get to be so cheesy?"

"It's a dad thing, man. I swear it changes your brain chemistry or something. Just wait, you'll see one day." As he said it, his face fell, and Gavin knew he was remembering the baby he'd almost had with Holly.

"It's okay," Gavin said, not allowing him to apologize. "Maybe someday I will. Though, I doubt it. My life isn't exactly kid-friendly."

"Well, let's take care of this dead body, and then we'll work on getting you a G-rating," Gunner said with a laugh. "Where is he?"

Gavin pulled his brother into a hug, ignoring the unusual way it felt. Gunner seemed shocked at first, though after a moment, he threw his arms around Gavin, patting him on the back.

"I've missed you, brother," Gavin said, burying his face in his older brother's neck. "I really have."

"I've missed you too, Gav," Gunner told him, squeezing his back before pulling away. "Now, grab the bleach from the trunk."

THE STREET LIGHT WAS ON, illuminating the small front lawn as Gavin, Gunner, Vaida, Cody, Sarah, and Joy crossed the dark street, carrying the supplies to erase any evidence of Vaida's crime.

Gavin was surprised that everyone wanted to help, but they all seemed to be fascinated by Gunner's old line of work. When they entered the house, Gavin was relieved not to be overwhelmed by the smell of death that Gunner often talked about. The smell that Holly had given off after a while before he had to leave her in the apartment. He couldn't remember how long it took to set in, but apparently a few hours wasn't long enough.

Vaida led the group into the bedroom where Riley's body lay. Gavin was surprised that his stomach held strong, despite not having seen a dead body since Holly's. Vaida wouldn't maintain eye contact with him, her face sullen. He reached out for her hand, squeezing it gently, though he was careful of her thumbs.

"Oh god," Cody said, making gagging noises as he covered his mouth. "I'm going to have to update my new roommate interview questions. Dead bodies are not on my list of fun times."

"Okay," Gunner said. "Let's get to work." He laid out a tarp on the ground. "We need to get him on here."

Cody, only using one hand as the other covered his nose, Gavin, and Gunner bent over, lifting Riley's thin body onto the clear tarp. Gunner rolled him over, wrapping the tarp around him and shoving the body out of the room. "I need towels," he instructed. "Like every towel you own."

Vaida disappeared from the room, returning a few moments later with a stack of towels. Gunner took them, wiping his forehead with the back of his arm. "It was a chest wound, so the lungs hold most of the blood, which is a good thing. Put on some gloves, Gav. You can help me soak up what we can. I'll use a box cutter to make sure it didn't soak through to the hardwood."

"And if it did?" Vaida asked.

"Depends on how long we have and how thorough we want to be. I can replace the floors, but it'll take a while. I can clean it up pretty well, though, with disinfectants and enzyme solvents."

Vaida nodded. "Do whatever you need to do." She paused, looking at Gavin. "There's, um, Noah's...well...there's more."

Gavin understood. "There's more to clean up in the living room," he told Gunner. "It was a head wound and it's a few months old."

"Shit," Gunner cursed.

Vaida frowned. "I'm so sorry."

"It's okay," Gunner said. "At least there are a lot of us to work. This is going to be a big job." He tossed Gavin a towel and handed a bucket of clear fluid to Vaida. "Go pour this on the stain. It's going to ruin the carpets, but we're going to have to cut them up anyway. We're going to need some putty knives, too. There should be some in my bag. If it was a head wound, it's going to be a pain. Brain matter is like concrete once it dries."

"I never thought a man talking about brains could be so hot," Joy whispered, making Sarah laugh.

"I can't believe you aren't freaked out by all of this," Vaida told Gunner.

"I used to do it for a living."

"No, I know that," she said. "But, you aren't the least bit hesitant to help me. You don't even know me."

"You make my brother happy," he said firmly. "That's all I need to know. As long as you're good to him, you're family, too. And if there's one thing you should know about this family...it's that dysfunctional as we may be, and trust me, we are, there isn't much we won't do for each other."

Vaida smiled. "Thank you, Gunner."

Gavin couldn't help swelling with pride at his brother's words as he scrubbed the carpet. Gunner bent down in front of him, taking a towel and helping to clean up the mess. "What are we going to do with the body?" he asked.

"Don't worry, brother. We always think of something."

THIRTY-SIX

VAIDA

Vaida, Sarah, and Joy were in the living room scrubbing the carpet, when a knock on the door sounded. They looked up, all eyes filled with fear.

"What do we do?" Sarah whispered.

"Shhh," Joy shushed her. Vaida stood, walking toward the door slowly. "Maggie, no," Joy warned, but she wasn't listening.

She lifted up on her tiptoes, peering out the small window in the top of the door and gasped. "Dani?" she asked, opening the door in a hurry.

Danielle shook her head, her eyes wide. "You're...you're home?"

She nodded, pulling her sister into a hug, her indiscretions forgotten for the moment. "I missed you so much," she told her, squeezing her tight.

Danielle seemed flabbergasted, her arms hanging loosely

at her sides before she lifted them to hug Vaida back. "I can't believe you're here," she said, sounding appalled. "You just...left. Without a word. You didn't say good-bye. Do you even know Noah left me? I haven't heard from him in months. I've been so alone," Danielle told her, her voice cracking. "I kept trying to call, but your phone was shut off."

"I'm so sorry," Vaida apologized, pulling away from her so she could meet her eyes. "Come inside, and I'll explain everything."

"Where's Riley?" she asked, looking through the door to where Joy and Sarah were. "What are they doing here?"

"Please just come inside, Dani, I'll explain it all."

"Explain what all? What are you talking about?" Her voice grew louder.

"Shh," Vaida warned her. "Please. Please just come inside. Just trust me, okay?"

"Trust you?" Danielle asked. "I don't even know you anymore, Maggie. You left me."

"I didn't," she said, tears clouding her vision at her sister's words. "I didn't leave you, Dani. I didn't have a choice."

"What are you talking about, you didn't have a choice? There's always a choice."

"No," Vaida told her. "Not for me." She pulled her sister's arm, but she jerked away.

"I'm not coming in there. Not until you tell me what in the hell is going on. You're not going to ambush me and guilt me into forgiving you just because you've brought them along," she said, gesturing toward Sarah and Joy. Her distressed voice was entirely too loud in the quiet neighborhood.

"Fine," Vaida held her hands up, trying to get her to lower her voice. "Let's go for a walk. We can talk alone. Just you and me."

Danielle thought for a moment before nodding hesitantly. "Okay, fine."

Vaida walked out the door, shutting it behind her. "I know I have a lot to explain to you."

"Yeah, you do," Danielle agreed, walking slowly beside her sister.

"Well, first of all, I go by Vaida now. After Grandma."

She furrowed her brow. "Why?"

"It's a long story," Vaida explained. "But, it all starts with Riley." She took a deep breath. "I don't know how much you know, but Riley was...he was very abusive to me."

Danielle stared at her sister, her voice filled with shock. "What?"

She nodded. "I'm sorry. I wanted to tell you, but I was embarrassed. And somehow I felt like it was what I deserved after Grandma died. Like, it was my punishment for all I put her through."

"That's insane," her sister said. "I'm so sorry I didn't know. I could kill him."

Vaida swallowed. "Well, I ran away. I couldn't take it anymore. I just...I just ran. And I knew that if I told you what happened, I'd be putting you in danger, too. So, I couldn't contact you. I didn't plan it, it's just how it happened, and I'm sorry you felt alone or ever had to worry about me."

Danielle stopped when they reached the backyard, hugging her sister. "No. You don't have to apologize. You...I mean, I completely understand why you did what you did. I can't imagine what you had to go through, how terrified you must've been. I'm so sorry I wasn't there for you."

Vaida nodded against her sister's collar bone. "I'm going to be okay now. I made friends in Atlanta. Friends who are helping me cope. And...I'm not afraid anymore."

"What are you going to do about Riley? Are you divorcing him?"

She closed her eyes. "I know about the two of you."

Danielle feigned ignorance. "What are you talking about?"

"I heard you...*together*. Riley found me in Atlanta. He brought me home and tied me up in the bedroom. That's where I was when you were with him last night."

She covered her mouth, her eyes watering. "Maggie, I'm so sorry. I didn't know. I thought you'd left. Riley made me believe that you and Noah had run off together and...he was the only one who seemed to understand how I was feeling. I had no idea what he was capable of. I would've never—"

"I know," Vaida responded. "Riley is really good at making you feel like the most important, most amazing thing in his life. When I fell for him, he was romantic and sweet and adventurous and...he made me feel alive when I had been feeling so out of it for the longest time. And when he is good, he is really, really good." She smiled sadly. "But when he is bad...there's no stopping him."

"So, what do we do?"

She swallowed. "I took care of him."

Her sister took a step back. "What do you mean you took care of him?"

"I had no choice, Danielle. None. I never wanted to...I never planned—" She stopped, closing her eyes and taking a breath to regain composure. "He left me no choice. He could've left me in Atlanta, but he wouldn't stop. He was never going to stop hunting me down. He'd never let me leave him. He was going to kill me. I did what I had to do."

"Meaning what?" Her sister clutched her chest, her eyes telling her she knew what Vaida meant.

"He's dead, Dani. He'll never hurt anyone again."

Danielle's legs went limp, and she fell to the ground, covering her mouth as sobs ripped through the silence of the night. She was hyperventilating, her hands shaking. Vaida bent down and engulfed her in a hug. "Breathe," she whispered. Her sister had had a similar panic attack after their grandmother's death. "Just breathe." She rocked her gently, taking her hands and placing them on the grass. It helped for her to feel something solid, something to ground her. "It's okay. It's all going to be okay."

Danielle looked up at her with dark eyes. "How can you say that? You're a murderer, Maggie. You killed someone." She pulled back from her sister. "I can't be here right now. I need to go."

"You're in no state to leave right now."

"What are you going to do? Tie me up? Are you going to do what you claim he did to you? How does that make you any better than him?"

"Of course I'm not going to tie you up, Dani. I just want to make sure you're safe. Just take a breath and please calm down. I don't want the neighbors to hear—" She stopped, her eyes traveling to several cinder blocks near the old shed. "What is that?" She stood up, leaving her sister on the ground and making her way to the pile.

She bent down. *Fresh dirt.* Something had been buried

here. Or rather, *someone.* Knowing she had found Noah's gravesite, but praying she was wrong, she grabbed the shovel Riley had left propped up against the side of the white shed. She pulled the heavy blocks off the pile, pressing the end of the shovel into the dirt and shoving down. She lifted the dirt and shoveled it slowly, both wanting to discover if she was right and dreading it at the same time.

When she made contact with something that didn't budge under her shovel, the smell hit her. "Oh, god," she said, covering her nose.

"What is it?" Danielle called from where she sat on the ground.

"Stay over there, Dani," Vaida warned, bending down and brushing the dirt from Noah's body. Her stomach began to rumble, but she pressed her teeth together firmly. "I'm so sorry," she whispered, lowering her head. "I'm so sorry this happened to you. It was all my fault." Her tears began falling, making little specks of mud in the dirt. She reached down, touching his bloated hand. The moon's glow lit up the grave just enough for her to know that it was him."I wish you could have a real grave. You deserve it." She frowned, knowing that for her plan to work, it could never happen. This would be his resting place. She could plant some flowers over him, give him some semblance of the tribute he deserved. "God bless you, Noah Tremble."

"*Noah*?" her sister's distraught voice called from behind her. She was standing only inches away, though Vaida hadn't noticed her approaching. She winced, unable to look at her sister.

"I'm so sorry, Dani. He was trying to help me. He knew about Riley. About how he was hurting me." She pushed some of the dirt back onto his body. "He came over to try to get me to leave, and Riley killed him. Without thinking twice. I wish you didn't have to see this. I shouldn't have dug him up. Not with you here. I just wanted to see if I was right. And I wanted to say goodbye. He was a hero. A true hero. He died trying to save me, and I'll never forgive myself for th —" She was rambling then, but stopped as her fingers came into contact with something else in the dirt. Something she hadn't noticed when she was digging. She pulled the small black box out of the grave, dusting it off. "What is this?" She popped the lid off with her thumb, staring down at two wedding rings. "Dani, why is your wedding ring in here?"

She looked to her side. The shovel was no longer where she left it.

"You should've stayed tied up," her sister's hate-filled voice whispered from just inches away.

THWACK.

Darkness.

THIRTY-SEVEN

DANIELLE
BEFORE

Danielle hurried into the kitchen, looking for the purse she'd purposefully left behind. She grabbed her ChapStick, rubbing it over her lips carefully as she waited for him.

As usual, within a few moments, he'd come to check on her. Also as usual, her dumb sister and clueless husband were just that: dumb and clueless. Riley hurried to her side, wrapping his arms around her and kissing her lips. His body warmed her in a way she was only warmed by him. His hands cradled her hips.

"Oh, you have no idea how bad I want you right now," he whispered, his lips on her ear.

"Take me," she dared him, rubbing her cheek against his.

He groaned, pulling back. "Don't tempt me, woman."

"They'd never even notice," she told him, clutching his shirt and kissing his neck.

"Oh, I'd make sure the whole neighborhood would notice," he promised, smacking her ass so that she squeaked.

"When do I get you for myself?" she whined.

"Soon enough," he told her. "You know I have a plan."

"Yeah, I know," she said.

"And you're sure you're okay with it? I mean, once we kill them...there's no going back."

She rolled her eyes. "Riley, she's the reason my grandmother, the only parent I ever knew, is dead. She has to pay for that. I'll never forgive her."

He kissed her again. "You're so sexy when you're talking revenge."

"Besides, Noah practically moons over her every day. They deserve to be together forever."

"Buried together, that is," he said with a laugh.

"Eh, semantics."

One more quick kiss, and then Riley rushed back into the living room where they'd left Noah and Maggie. Danielle was getting tired of waiting.

AFTER NOAH LEFT *the house the next day, Danielle called Riley. "He's on his way to your house," she told him. "He'll be checking on Maggie. We can do this now."*

"Now?" Riley asked. "The plan wasn't supposed to happen for a few months."

"I know, but this works too, right?" He sighed. "Don't you want to be with me already?" she demanded.

"Of course I do, baby," he said dotingly. After a moment,

he went on. "Okay, I'll make it work. You're sure about this, right?"

"I've never been more sure," she said. "Oh, and Riley?"

"Yeah, babe?"

"Make it hurt."

THIRTY-EIGHT

DANIELLE
AFTER

The months after Maggie left were the happiest of her life. Finally, after years of waiting, Danielle had Riley all to herself, so the day that he found Maggie and went after her was utterly devastating. She'd never felt more betrayed.

When he brought her home, Danielle made sure their love-making was the loudest it'd ever been. She wanted her sister to hear every moment she spent with the man Maggie could never again have to herself. She wouldn't allow Riley to forget the plan. The pact they'd made. A spouse for a spouse. She'd paid her price, so why was his spouse still breathing? Hers was buried in the backyard, and yet he was still living with Maggie. It wasn't fair.

When she'd come over that night and Maggie opened the door, it had been the final gut punch. No, scratch that, finding out Riley was dead...having to listen to Maggie's pitiful *oh-woe-is-me* story was the final gut punch. And then the fact that she'd chosen to take on Vaida's name. A woman who had died because of the life-altering depression her own granddaughter had caused. There was no name for the amount of rage that filled Danielle's stomach as she allowed her sister to comfort her, to pretend it was helping.

She watched as she dug up Noah's grave, blissfully unaware that it would soon be her own. When she'd found the body, Danielle knew it was time to make her move. She crawled toward her, swiping the shovel without notice. When Maggie found the rings, she stood up, holding the shovel above her head, ready to swing.

And then, just like that, she did. THWACK. There had never been a more satisfying sound than the crunch of metal against her sister's skull. She watched as Maggie's body crumpled into the grave, landing on top of Noah with a soft thud. She smiled down through her tears. Riley may be gone, but she'd exacted vengeance upon his killer. Her final act for the one she'd love forever.

She scooped up a pile of dirt, dumping it onto their bodies. And then another. Again and again she poured the dirt onto them, watching as the earth swallowed them up.

And then, out of nowhere, there was pain. Oh, so much pain. Danielle bent over, clutching her stomach. She pulled her hand away, looking at the thick blood that coated her fingers. She'd been shot. No, there was no sound. Stabbed, maybe? She fell to the ground, trying to catch her breath. It felt as though all the oxygen had been sucked from the sky, no amount of breaths were enough.

Her vision blurred as she ran out of air and a dark figure stood over her. *Who are you?* she wanted to ask the person above her. *What have you done?* Instead, she drifted off to sleep, knowing she'd never wake again.

THIRTY-NINE

GAVIN

The bedroom was cleaned and scrubbed, the carpet had been cut up, and the hardwood was disinfected. The brothers were drenched in sweat as they carried the body into the living room with Cody's help, setting it down without caution.

"How's it coming, ladies?" Gunner asked.

Sarah and Joy smiled up at him, shamelessly flirting. "Good, boss," Sarah said. "We didn't have to scrape too much from the hardwood. Most of the, um, *brain matter,* was trapped in the carpet so we could just cut it out."

"Excellent," Gunner said, walking over to examine their work. He poured a little extra disinfectant and bent down to help scrub. Both ladies leaned back, admiring his work. "It looks like you guys got it all. Did Vaida want to try and pull up these floors? Or just leave them? There's going to be some ingrained into the wood that we probably can't get."

"Um, I don't know," Gavin answered, looking around. "Where is Vaida?"

"She went outside with Danielle a while ago," Joy said.

"Danielle? Her sister?"

"She came by," Sarah said. "They wanted to talk alone."

"How long's it been?" Gavin asked, feeling uneasy.

"A while," Joy answered, looking at the clock on the wall.

"I'm going to go check on them," he said. "Ladies, can one of you pull Cody's car into the garage?"

"My car?" Cody asked. "Uh-uh, I ain't no dead guy transportation service," he said, sounding appalled.

"We'll load him into mine," Gunner said. "We can take him out on one of the boats. Weigh him down and drop him a few hundred miles from here."

Gavin nodded, walking out the door as the group began cleaning up the supplies. Vaida wasn't outside, so he made his way to Sarah and Joy's house. "Vaida? You in here?" he called. No answer. He turned around, hurrying back toward the house.

Where could she be? He hurried around the side of the house to the backyard, gasping as he saw a pile of loose dirt. *No.*

The area around him smelled. It was the same smell Holly's body had made, and he knew what would be waiting for him under the dirt. He rushed toward it, using his hands to dig feverishly. Within moments, he saw her face and let out a cry. "*No, no, no,*" he said, pushing the rest of the dirt from her chest and climbing into the shallow grave to pull her up. He laid her on the ground outside the grave, listening for a heartbeat. The crickets and buzzing from the street lights were suddenly the loudest they'd ever been. Was she breathing? He couldn't tell. Panic was setting in as he lifted her chin up, trying to remember what he'd seen on tv. He placed his mouth over hers, pushing a breath of air into her mouth. He watched her chest rise. That was a good sign, right? It wasn't supposed to move her stomach, he remembered that much. Should he pump her chest? Was it three pumps or five? There was a song he could pump to...what was it? He put his mouth on hers again, breathing hard. There was blood on the side of her scalp that had rubbed onto his cheek.

He put his hands onto her chest, praying he'd manage to save her and not make it worse. He pumped once, twice, three times. Was that enough? Another breath. More pumps. Why the hell hadn't he been a lifeguard as a teen? He'd once had the body for it. Oh, wait. Scars.

His thoughts were wild and jumbled as he pushed on her chest, breathing air into her when it seemed like her chest hadn't moved in too long. Finally, he sat back, pulling his knees into his chest and giving in to the sobs that he'd been holding back. He rubbed a dirt covered hand over his eyes, smearing mud through his tears. He couldn't lose her. He just couldn't. "Please, Vaida," he begged. "Please. I can't lose you again. Not again." He leaned down once more, rubbing the blood from her head and pulling her into his arms, cradling her carefully. "Please," he cried again. "Please don't die on me."

After a few heart wrenching, earth shattering moments, he heard her take a breath. He wasn't sure he'd heard it, or if it was his head playing tricks on him, but then there was another one. He looked down into his arms as her eyes fluttered open. "Gavin?" she asked, coughing loudly. He sat her up, smacking her back to help her cough up the dirt that escaped her throat. When her coughing stopped, he hugged her, laughing loudly as he grew overwhelmed with happiness. He kissed her, his mouth firm against hers, one hand in her hair.

"Are you okay?" he asked, moving the hair back from the bloody sore on her temple. "What happened?"

She shook her head, touching the wound and wincing. She looked down at her fingers, rubbing the blood on her pants. "It was...my sister. She attacked me."

"Your sister?" he asked. "But why?"

"She was in love with Riley. I found her wedding bands in Noah's grave. She'd known he was dead all along. Riley had her fooled. He was good at that," she said, sitting up with a painful sigh. "Where is she?" she asked.

"Your sister?" He looked around. "I have no idea. She wasn't here when I got here. We need to get you to a hospital."

"No," she said firmly. "Not until—" She stopped, coughing again. "Not until we cover up Noah's grave. He deserves to be buried with some dignity."

"But, you could be really hurt."

"I'm fine," she said, rubbing her head again. "Please just help me bury him. Then we can leave this place and never come back."

Finally, Gavin gave in. "I'll do it," he agreed. "You just sit there. When we're done, we can bury Riley back here, too." He looked at the small shed. "Can this be moved?"

Vaida looked at it. "I don't know."

"I have an idea," he said. "It's crazy."

"I think I've heard that before. What do you need?"

He thought for a moment, excited to use the part of his brain that had always enjoyed figuring out mechanical things. It was something he hadn't had much opportunity to do anymore. "Do you have a car jack? Like to fix a flat tire?"

"Sure, yeah. Riley would've had one around here somewhere."

"I'll need that and some pipes."

"Okay," she said, sitting up. "I'll see what I can find."

"Oh, and some two-by-fours, too. If you can find them."

"There should be some in the shed, actually. There was always some new project Riley was going to start working on."

"Good," Gavin said, picking up the shovel from the ground and beginning to cover the body. "If we can make this work, we'll at least make it harder for anyone to find their bodies. It should give us more time to get away."

She smiled at him. "Thanks, Gavin. I owe you...so much more than one."

AN HOUR LATER, both bodies had been buried and the group was working to get the shed hoisted up. On the back end, they had jacked it up high enough to place a few pieces of wood underneath it. Now, they had the jack holding the front up as they'd laid the longest two-by-fours down, placing the PVC pipe Vaida had found underneath it, one in the middle and one near the front.

"Okay," Gavin said, wiping his forehead with his arm. "Now, we just lower the front down. Slowly. And if it works, we should be able to push it forward and over the graves."

The group formed a circle around the building. "Watch your toes," Gavin warned.

At the front, Gunner lowered the jack and Gavin held his breath, waiting to see if the pipes would hold the weight of the shed. When they didn't crack, he nodded. "Okay, now push it forward slowly," he said, easing it forward. "Now, someone grab that pipe from the back and move it to the front." Cody did as he was told, grabbing the pipe and moving it. With one final shove, the shed was where they needed it to be. "Now, everyone stay where you are. Gunner and I will jack it back up and get the pipes and wood out from under it."

"This was genius," Vaida said.

Gavin lowered his head. "No big deal."

He walked with his brother as Gunner placed the jack under the building and allowed him to pull the pipes and wood out from under it before lowering it back to the ground. They stepped away, dusting off their hands, and Gavin couldn't help but feel proud. He'd done it. He'd finally saved the girl.

FORTY

GAVIN

The next day, the brothers stood outside of Gunner's home, saying their good-byes. "I don't know when I'll see you again," Gavin told him.

"I know," Gunner said, hugging him close.

"I'll keep in touch when I can."

"Same here," Gunner said. "Joy and Sarah will reach out if they see the police snooping around the house. I'll give you a call. That will give you guys time to get further away."

"We did a good job of cleaning up," Gavin said. "I have you to thank for that."

"It was your idea to cover the bodies. And to lay the tools and wood on the spot where the shed was. You thought of everything. That's what will save her in the end."

"It was a team effort," Gavin said.

"Hey, I want to give you something. And I don't want you to fight me on it, okay?" Gunner asked.

"A black eye?"

"No," he said seriously, sliding a wad of cash into Gavin's palm. Gavin looked down, his eyes wide.

"What is this for?"

"You need a car," he said. "You were smart not to take Vaida's, but once you take Cody back to Atlanta, you'll be stranded again. I never knew you sold your car to pay for Gia's care. That wasn't fair to you."

"Who else was going to do it?" he asked with a shrug. "You don't have to give me this. I've got some money put back. We'll be okay."

"I know you will," Gunner told him. "I know. But, this is just to make sure. It's five thousand. Not enough to get anything great, but work is good right now. I'm doing okay." He nodded. "I want to do this. For you. Because I care about what happens to you, Gav. I know we don't talk like this much, but I care. And I know you haven't really had anyone around to tell you that lately. The money's yours. You can do whatever you want to with it. But, you need a reliable car."

Gavin nodded, looking away and sliding the cash into his pocket. "I don't know what to say."

"Just promise you'll call."

"I will," he said, looking up to smile at Vaida as she and Reagan walked out of the house. "You ready?" he asked her.

She grinned, squeezing Reagan's hand. "You have to bring her back," Reagan said. "I hardly got to meet her, and now you're running off again."

"We'll be back," Gavin promised. "Just as soon as we can." He patted his pocket. "Seriously, Gunner, thank you."

"You guys be safe, okay?" Gunner asked. "That's the most important thing."

"We'll be fine," he said as Gunner ruffled his hair.

"Don't make me come looking for you."

"I promise we'll keep in touch." With one last hug, Gavin and Vaida climbed into the car. "Thanks again for everything."

"Any time, brother," Gunner said with a nod. "Take care of him," he told Vaida.

"Will do," she said. "Thank you both."

"It was nice to meet you, Cody," Gunner told him, patting the window.

"I hope I never have to see you again," Cody said, and Gavin was pretty sure he was only half-kidding. They waved as they pulled from the driveway in Cody's car.

"Cody, have you changed your mind about road tripping with us?" Vaida asked, looking to the backseat.

"I am in the backseat of my own car," Cody said. "I've spent the past twenty-four hours of my life in enough stress to give me a hernia and enough crime to send me away for the rest of my life. Just because I'm gay doesn't mean gay prison sex is appealing to me," he said, his voice shrill. He laid his head on the seat and closed his eyes. "I love you both, but I was wrong before when I said I wanted to know more about you. I'm good. I don't need to know anything else." His hands waved wildly in the air as he rambled. "Your lives belong on an HBO show, not in the front seat of my car."

"Fair enough," Gavin said.

"And it's about time you got your own car," Cody said. "Don't be guilting me into giving you this one. Bessie and I have been through some good times."

"Don't worry," Vaida said. "You've done more than enough."

"You're damn right I have," he said, pursing his lips and crossing his arms. "Burying dead bodies. What am I? Do I look like a grave digger to you? Gold digger, maybe. Grave digger? Hell, no."

FORTY-ONE

VAIDA

Back at the apartment in Atlanta, Vaida was staring around the nearly empty bedroom. Cody stood in the doorway. "I'm really going to miss you around here," he told her, pulling her into another hug.

"I'll miss you, too," she agreed. "Thank you for taking a chance on me. You saved my life."

He nodded, a sad smile on his face. "You saved mine, too —nah, mine was already pretty great. But, you definitely made it interesting."

She laughed. "You'll have to keep me updated on *Drop Dead Diva*. I'll never know if Jane and Grayson end up together."

"What I want to know is if you two will end up together," he said. "You've got a good one there, Vaida. Not many men would do everything he did for you."

"I know," she said. "I plan to keep him."

"Good," he said. "'Cause, frankly, he knows too much, and there isn't enough room under that shed for anyone else." He shook his head, squeezing her again. "Y'all are going to get a car, right?"

"Yes," she told him. "Right after this."

"Do you need any money?"

She touched his hand. "You've done more than enough for some strange girl who walked into your bar. I'm going to be fine, Cody. I promise you."

"Just...take care of yourself. And, if you're ever back in town, you've always got somewhere to crash."

"Noted." She smiled. "I hope your next roommate is as entertaining as me," she said as she headed toward the door.

"Don't wish that on anyone, boo-boo," he said, holding the door open as she walked out. "I'll see you when I see you."

"See you when I see you," she said, trying not to let him see the tears in her eyes.

FORTY-TWO

GAVIN

Gavin picked out a black truck similar to the one he'd driven as a teenager, loading the few things he owned into it and driving out of town with the woman he loved beside him. Love. It was a funny concept, considering they'd only known each other a few months, but going through so much together forced him to realize how true it was.

He hadn't said it yet, not wanting to scare her away. Though, truth be told, if neither of them were scared off yet, he doubted there'd be very much that could spook them.

"So, where do you want to live?" he asked her.

"Anywhere you are," she told him, scooting closer to him in the truck's seat.

He kissed her head. "We'll go to New York first and get your new ID. Ryan is getting it ready for us now. But, after that, we can go anywhere you want."

"And everywhere we want."

"Exactly," he told her, lacing his fingers through hers.

"After everything bad we've been through, we deserve some happiness. And some fun."

"I don't think anyone deserves as much happiness as you give me, Maggie-Vaida Harris-Williams." He slowed down at the red light, pulling her face up to his and kissing her, allowing himself to lose his senses in her kiss. She warmed his chest, filling a space he thought Holly's death had left empty forever.

She kissed him twice more, snuggling her head onto his shoulder as the light changed. "You do, Gavin-Fletcher James-Denali. You deserve every happiness this world has to give." She rubbed her hand over his. "And I'm going to do everything I can to make sure you get it."

He squeezed her palm, minding her broken thumb. "I was right before. We're a match made in heaven, aren't we?" he asked.

"I don't think heaven has much to do with us," she told him, shaking her head. "Brokenness, crime, adultery, fake identities...something tells me our love isn't heaven's type."

He laid his head over onto hers. There was that word again: love. "Well, lucky for us, our love is my type. My perfect, beautiful, amazing type." He kissed her hand. "I wouldn't have it any other way." And then they were kissing as he drove down the empty road, one eye on the windshield and one closed and lost in Vaida. Everything about their story was dangerous, messy, and disastrous...why change that now?

EPILOGUE

GAVIN

TWO MONTHS LATER

Gavin stared at the apartment wall, cocking his head to one side and then the other. "I don't know. I still don't think it's even."

Vaida walked into the room, two mugs of cocoa in her hands. "It's fine, babe," she told him, stepping up onto the couch and kissing his cheek before sitting down, careful not to spill. "I put extra ice in yours."

He set the drill down, claiming one of the mugs and taking a sip. He set it down on the table, rolling his eyes as Vaida quickly moved it to a coaster. "I just want it to be perfect for you," he said. "It's the only picture we have of you and your grandmother."

"And the only picture we have of you and your siblings," Vaida told him. "And I think they're perfectly even."

Gavin picked up the last frame from the shelf, a picture of him and Vaida they'd had made on their first night in their new hometown of London, Louisiana. He grabbed the drill, screwing a hole into the middle and hanging the frame. "Now, it's perfect."

He sat down on the couch, and she threw her legs over his lap, looking around the apartment they were slowly making look like a home. He rubbed her legs. "I love you," she said, looking at him.

"I love you, too," he said.

"I know." She smiled, sliding over onto his lap and setting her mug on the end table. "I like our life, Gavin James."

"I like our life, too, Vaida James." He grinned back at her, and she kissed him firmly, her hands in the hair that had grown so long.

"I like the sound of that," she told him.

"Oh yeah? Wanna do something about it?" he asked, an eyebrow raised.

"I wish," she said. "I wish I could take your real name."

"Me too," he told her, brushing a piece of hair from her eyes. "Trust me, I do." He kissed her nose. "But, that doesn't mean you can't have it. To me, anyway. We may not ever be able to get legally married because, ya know, the whole being dead thing makes it difficult—but you've been mine, and I've been yours from the moment I laid eyes on you."

"Ooh, with the lines," she teased.

"I'm serious," he said. "Marriage is just a piece of paper anyway. The commitment, we already have that. We can do the ceremony. We can definitely do the honeymoon," he told her, his pants growing tighter as she kissed him again. "I want you to be my wife, Vaida, and just because the state of Louisiana can't recognize it doesn't mean I can't."

She nodded. "How did I get so lucky?" she asked, pecking her lips onto his.

The beard he'd been growing scratched her as he answered. "Even the most unlucky get lucky sometimes."

"I think we should get lucky right now," she said, lowering her voice as her mouth moved toward his ear.

"Oh yeah?" he said, lifting her up and walking toward the bedroom. She laughed out loud, though they both fell deadly silent as a knock on the door interrupted them. He gently set her down on her feet, his eyes locked on the long hallway to their door.

Without looking to Vaida, he hurried down the hall and grabbed the metal baseball bat they kept behind the triple-locked door. No one had ever knocked on their door, nor had there been any reason to. And, despite their attempts at normalcy, they both knew their life would never be what most people considered normal. Anyone who would be looking for them wouldn't be bringing them good news.

Gavin opened the door, bat in the air, and stared into his brother's face. "Gunner?" he asked, lowering the bat instantly, the adrenaline draining from him. "What on earth are you doing here?"

"We have a problem," Gunner said, ushering Nora, Duncan, and Reagan into the apartment without being asked in. They were each carrying bags and wearing worried expressions.

"What's going on?" Vaida asked, moving toward them.

Gunner pulled out a paper from his pocket, unfolding it quickly. "It's Gia," he said grimly. "She's out."

Gavin looked down to the paper, dread filling his belly as he stared at his sister's handwriting.

She was going to kill her. I took care of it.

Keep reading for a sneak peek of:

The Prisoner, The Messes Series Book Four
The epic finale...

CHAPTER ONE

FIONA

They believed she was a monster. And, she guessed, maybe she was. All she knew was that she'd done what she had to do. To survive. To protect herself. To protect them.

Fiona Denali drove the bustling interstate with a vacant mind. The radio in her beat up car didn't work, but that was okay. She liked silence. Preferred it, in fact. It left her mind free to wander. The gas light on the dash lit up and she frowned, searching for the next exit sign. She'd just crossed over into Tennessee, a state she'd briefly called home at one point, hoping to get lost in a busier city than the one she'd left.

As the exit ramp approached, she switched lanes, pressing her brake slightly. She let out a sigh as she saw the gas prices. The money she'd made in the last city was dwindling. She'd have to stop soon in order to make some more.

Settle down for a bit, but never for long. That was her rule. She had to keep moving, keep pressing on.

She pulled into the gas station, parked next to a pump, and climbed out of the car. She took a deep breath, stretching her arms above her head. When she walked into the building, she pulled out the tiny black wallet she carried, laying a one hundred dollar bill on the counter. The attendant stared at her. "We can't take that," he said.

"What do you mean you can't take it?" she asked, already irritated with his whiny voice and cystic acne.

He pointed to a blue sign beside the register that read,

Attendant Accepts Bills $20 and Under.

She groaned. "I don't have anything else."

"I'm sorry," he said, clearly not sorry. "It's policy."

"What kind of shit policy is that? I need gas and I have cash. Why the hell can't you take my hundred? Hold it up to the light or whatever. It's fine," she said, shoving the bill closer to him.

He pushed it back. "I'm sorry," he repeated. "You'll have to come back with something smaller."

"I don't have anything smaller. And I need gas now. You're the only station at this exit."

He shrugged. "I need you to step aside, so I can help the next customer."

"Are you serious right now? You're turning away a paying customer."

His face remained expressionless. "I don't make the rules, lady. Next," he called, looking to the man standing behind her.

She snatched the money from the counter, muttering under her breath and storming out of the building, boiling with rage. She walked to her car, staring around. It was no use. There hadn't been another station on the sign and she could see for miles on the flat stretch of highway. She groaned, climbing into her car and placing her head on the steering wheel. She tried to think, quickly, of what she could do. There was nowhere around to break her bill. She could try and get a random customer to give her the change, but what were the chances of that? She certainly wouldn't do it if the situation were reversed. Knowing her luck, the person would end up running off with her money.

A knock on her window caused her to jump. She lifted her head, looking over. There was a man standing outside of her car. He wore a flannel shirt and a beanie on his head; curly, chin-length brown hair framed his face. She leaned over, turning the window crank so it would lower just a bit. "Yeah?" she asked.

"Hi," he said sheepishly. "Sorry if I startled you. I heard your, erm, encounter with the attendant. I wanted to see if I could help."

"Really?" she asked, feeling skeptical. "Why?"

"You looked like you could use it," he said, shrugging. "Thank you." She nodded. "If you could just break this

hundred, you'd really be doing me a favor." She held out the bill.

"Actually, I wanted to see if you could do me one in return," he said, his breath fogging up the crisp fall air.

Her heart sank, knowing it couldn't have been that easy. "What do you want?" she asked, eyeing him. She hadn't always been above doing *anything* for cash, but she'd made a vow to herself that she'd be better than that. Or at least try. She had to find her morals again. Whatever they may be.

"I need to get away from here," he told her. "I'll pay for your gas in exchange for you taking me with you."

"Taking you with me? You have no idea where I'm headed."

"I'm not headed anywhere specific," he said. "Wherever you can take me. However far you want. I have money, and I'll keep your tank full as long as you're willing to have me tag along."

"Why?" she asked.

"Just looking for a change of scenery," he said. She knew he was lying but, honestly, what choice did she have? It was a hard offer to pass up.

"Okay," she said finally.

"Yeah?" he asked, seeming shocked.

She nodded. "Go fill me up."

"Uh, you have to come with me," he told her.

"Why should I?" she asked, looking around to check and see if someone was waiting for her to step out of the car so they could steal it. She was paranoid, she knew, but life had made her that way and it kept her safe.

"Because I'm not going to go pay for your gas and let you drive away with it and leave me here."

She shook her head. She hadn't thought of doing that. Why hadn't she thought of doing that? "I'm not going to steal from you," she said.

"How would I know that?"

"How do I know you aren't a serial killer?"

"Fair enough," he said, nodding his head. "Tell you what, I'll trust you if you'll trust me."

"Sounds like a fair trade," she said, not telling him there was no way in hell she was going to trust him.

"Okay," he said, studying her face. "You aren't going to leave me?"

"No," she said, "I'm not going to leave." No need to tell him she was planning to use him for the free gas and kick him to the curb first chance she got. He nodded, walking away but continuing to watch her over his shoulder. She got out of the car, ready to pump the gas once he'd given her the okay.

She didn't like this idea. Traveling with a complete stranger. Time had taught her she couldn't even trust those she was closest to, so this was surely off limits. Still, desperate as she currently was, she didn't have room to be picky. Besides, if nothing else, Fiona was savvy. She could take care of herself. Always had. She was going to make sure this little arrangement worked to her benefit. If anyone was going to be double crossed, it wouldn't be her.

Ready to read the epic conclusion to The Messes Series? The Prisoner, The Messes Series #4, is available now!

ACKNOWLEDGMENTS

Thank you so much for reading the third book in The Messes Series: The Liar.

I hope you enjoyed reading Fletcher and Vaida's story as much as I enjoyed telling it! The connection these two had was unlike anything I've ever written and I know they'll always have a special place in my heart.

Speaking of special places in my heart, I have so many people to thank for helping me bring this book to the world!

First, to *my husband*, Michael, for always loving and supporting me. And bringing me ice cream when my characters are being particularly moody.

To *my family*, my parents, sisters, grandparents, many aunts and uncles, and my daughter, for supporting me from day one. You guys believed in me long before anyone else knew my name. Thanks for instilling hope into a little girl with dreams as big as the sky.

To *my PA* Brittany, is this really book four in our career together?! Holy cow! I am so thankful for all you do for me. For being the one to hear all my crazy ideas first, for believing in me when I'm struggling to believe in myself. I am forever grateful for the team we've built. You.Are.Awesome!

To *my betas*, Brittany, Holly, Kim, Kaitie, and Janise,

thank you for looking through all the mess of my first draft and helping clear away the clutter to find the beautiful story hidden within. Y'all are the best!

To *my Twisted Readers and Street Team,* thank you for supporting me every day and in every endeavour. Our little group has grown to feel like a family and I don't know what I'd do without you all!

To *Joy Westerfield, Sarah DeLong, and Danielle Harris,* readers who won a chance to make an appearance in this story. I hope you all had a blast learning about your namesakes. I had so much fun bringing all three of you to life in Fletcher's story. Joy and Sarah, sisters in heart & in print, I loved your sassy, fun characters. I'm sure they're somewhere drinking a glass of wine right now and dreaming about Gunner. They were a resounding force of good and without their help, this story wouldn't exist. Danielle, your character was certainly something to talk about. The twists and turns that went into her storyline were unexpected but a blast to play out. I hope you enjoyed the ride!

To *Kim Williams,* for helping me perfect Vaida. I can't thank you enough for helping me to bring a character who's been in my heart for so long to life.

To *my editor,* Sarah West from Three Owls Editing, thank you for whipping this book into shape. As always, your insights and suggestions were spot on and helped make this book a thousand times better.

To *everyone who has followed this series,* thank you! Thank you for believing in my characters and their stories. Thank you for falling in love with them like I have. Thank you for continuing to buy and spread the word about my beautiful messes.

To *my PR team at IndieSage*, thank you for working to get this book into as many hands as possible. Your tireless efforts are something to be revered. I couldn't do it without you!

And lastly, *to everyone who read and enjoyed this third installment of The Messes*, thank you for supporting me! I truly hope this story meant as much to you as it did to me. Good art is supposed to make us feel something, and I hope this book did that. Good, bad, or ugly—if this story evoked any emotion from you, I have done my job.

If this is your first experience with one of my books, I sincerely hope you'll hurry to grab the others. If this is just one of many of my books that you've read, thank you for continuing to follow me on this crazy journey. I hope this book was everything you've come to expect from my books and a total surprise all at once.

LETTER TO MY READERS

Dear Reader,

Thank you for reading The Liar (The Messes, #3).

I want to talk about domestic violence for a second. This book took on a very hard topic, but one that I hope you agree needs to be talked about. I chose to spend the vast majority of the month of October writing and researching for this book. If you don't know, October is National Domestic Violence Awareness Month, so it seemed fitting that this story came to life during that month.

In doing my research for this story, I talked with several domestic violence survivors who have escaped abusive situations. The biggest thing they mentioned to me was how terrifying it was to take that step and decide to get out.

If you or someone you know is dealing with a situation similar to what Vaida or Fletcher went through, I hope this book and these stories will give you the strength to seek help.

The domestic violence hotline is a fantastic resource that I hope you'll utilize if you ever need it.

Ph: 1-800-799-7233.

Or visit their website: https://www.thehotline.org/

Please know that you are not alone and that help is available to you.

All my love,

Kiersten Modglin

ABOUT THE AUTHOR

KIERSTEN MODGLIN is an Amazon Top 10 bestselling author of psychological thrillers and a member of International Thriller Writers, Novelists, Inc., and the Alliance of Independent Authors. Kiersten is a KDP Select All-Star and a recipient of *ThrillerFix*'s Best Psychological Thriller Award, *Suspense Magazine*'s Best Book of 2021 Award, a 2022 Silver Falchion for Best Suspense, and a 2022 Silver Falchion for Best Overall Book of 2021. She grew up in rural western Kentucky and later relocated to Nashville, Tennessee, where she now lives with her husband, daughter, and their two Boston terriers: Cedric and Georgie. Kiersten's work is currently being translated into multiple languages and readers across the world refer to her as 'The Queen of Twists.' A Netflix addict, Shonda Rhimes superfan, psychology fanatic, and *indoor* enthusiast, Kiersten enjoys rainy days spent with her nose in a book.

Sign up for Kiersten's newsletter here:
kierstenmodglinauthor.com/nlsignup

Sign up for text alerts from Kiersten here:
kierstenmodglinauthor.com/textalerts

kierstenmodglinauthor.com
www.facebook.com/kierstenmodglinauthor
www.facebook.com/groups/kmodsquad
www.twitter.com/kmodglinauthor
www.instagram.com/kierstenmodglinauthor
www.tiktok.com/@kierstenmodglinauthor
www.goodreads.com/kierstenmodglinauthor
www.bookbub.com/authors/kiersten-modglin
www.amazon.com/author/kierstenmodglin

ALSO BY KIERSTEN MODGLIN

STANDALONE NOVELS

Becoming Mrs. Abbott

The List

The Missing Piece

Playing Jenna

The Beginning After

The Better Choice

The Good Neighbors

The Lucky Ones

I Said Yes

The Mother-in-Law

The Dream Job

The Nanny's Secret

The Liar's Wife

My Husband's Secret

The Perfect Getaway

The Roommate

The Missing

Just Married

Our Little Secret

Widow Falls

Missing Daughter

The Reunion

Tell Me the Truth

The Dinner Guests

If You're Reading This...

A Quiet Retreat

ARRANGEMENT TRILOGY

The Arrangement (Book 1)

The Amendment (Book 2)

The Atonement (Book 3)

THE MESSES SERIES

The Cleaner (The Messes, #1)

The Healer (The Messes, #2)

The Liar (The Messes, #3)

The Prisoner (The Messes, #4)

NOVELLAS

The Long Route: A Lover's Landing Novella

The Stranger in the Woods: A Crimson Falls Novella